Joseph Roth, c. 1932

JOSEPH ROTH was born in Brody, Galicia – then part of
Austria-Hungary and now in Ukraine – in 1894. He served
in the Austrian Army between 1916 and 1918 and worked
as a journalist from 1923 to 1932 in Berlin and Vienna.
When the Nazis came to power in 1933 he emigrated to
Paris, where he drank himself into an early grave in 1939.

Roth also wrote *The Antichrist*, *The Hundred Days*,
Weights and Measures, *Flight Without End* and *The Silent
Prophet*, which have also been published by Peter Owen,
as well as *The Radetzky March*, *String of Pearls* and *The
Legend of the Holy Drinker*.

ABOUT THE TRANSLATOR

Richard Panchyk is the author, editor or translator of twenty-three books, including *World War II for Kids*, *German New York City*, *Forgotten Tales of Long Island* and *Keys to American History*, as well as a study on Jewish assimilation and name change in the Austrian Empire during the nineteenth century. He produced a new translations of *The Antichrist* and *The Hundred Days* by Joseph Roth – to whom he is distantly related – both of which were published by Peter Owen.

PERLEFTER

The Story of a Bourgeois

Joseph Roth

PERLEFTER

The Story of a Bourgeois

Translated from the German by Richard Panchyk

PETER OWEN
London and Chicago

PETER OWEN PUBLISHERS
81 Ridge Road, London N8 9NP

Peter Owen books are distributed in the USA and Canada by
Independent Publishers Group/Trafalgar Square
814 North Franklin Street, Chicago, IL 60610, USA

Translated from the German *Perlefter: Die Geschichte eines Burger*
First published by Kiepenheuer & Witsch 1978

This translation first published in Great Britain by
Peter Owen Publishers 2013
Translation © Richard Panchyk 2013
Introduction © Richard Panchyk 2013

ISBN 978-0-7206-1487-9

A catalogue record for this book is available
from the British Library.

Printed and bound in Great Britain by
CPI Group (UK) Ltd, Croydon, CR0 4YY

Typeset by Octavo-Smith Ltd
in Constantia 11.5/15
Display Engravers MT

TRANSLATOR'S NOTE

While I was hard at work translating Joseph Roth's *The Hundred Days* I vowed it would be my last Roth translation. But all the while the question lurked in the back of my mind – dare I attempt one final challenge? Should I take on *Perlefter*? Was it a worthwhile endeavour? Indeed, it existed in German, but the effort required by Kiepenheuer & Witsch to publish it was limited to deciphering and transcribing Roth's longhand. Translation is another story entirely.

Was this partial manuscript, one that Roth had abandoned ten years before he died, one that was probably between halfway and two-thirds completed, worthy of publication in English? It helped somewhat knowing that Roberto Bravo de la Varga had deemed it a worthy project to translate *Perlefter* into Spanish (published in 2006 together with *Strawberries*, which, incidentally, also features a character named Napthali Kroj). Was there anything inherently wrong with translating an unfinished work?

The first thing that came to mind as I considered the latter question was Franz Kafka, who had instructed that all his manuscripts be burned after his death. Max

Brod ignored his instructions, and only because of that do we have Kafka's rich literary legacy available to us today. But Roth, unlike Kafka, was a successful writer during his lifetime, with many books to his credit and an established literary reputation. Would *Perlefter* contribute anything positive to the existing Roth *oeuvre* in English? I began to read the book, and I soon discovered that the answer was a resounding yes.

It is impossible to know how much refinement and revision the existing chapters of *Perlefter* would have gone through had the book been finished. The mere fact that it remained unfinished means that the previous question may be moot. A sort of 'what-if' line of questioning that can only lead to frustration. In effect, every translator is an editor, negotiating the nuances between two languages and making the transition as smooth as possible. But a translator's challenge is even greater than usual with such a manuscript. A translator must strive to bring a work into its new language with elegance and style to make it readable and digestible without completely rewriting or changing the meaning. So any curt or cryptic moments had to remain so. The published German book as it stands is certainly surprisingly cohesive, but there are clearly moments when the narrative feels rushed and dismissive or lacking in detail, as if parts of *Perlefter* were more or less an outline. I have not crossed any lines here, in the translation of this unfinished book. I have approached the project the same way that I approached my other two Roth translations – to create the English version of Roth's distinct voice.

I would like to thank Peter Owen and Antonia Owen for their belief in this important project, as well as Simon Smith, my excellent editor, and Michael O'Connell.

INTRODUCTION

Joseph Roth's (1894–1939) prodigious output included numerous novels, novellas, short stories and newspaper articles in the space of only sixteen years between 1923 and 1939. Born Moses Joseph Roth of Jewish parentage in the town of Brody, Galicia (present-day Ukraine), about fifty-four miles north-east of present-day Lviv (then called Lemberg), Roth was a product of the Austro-Hungarian Empire who first lived in Vienna then moved to Berlin. After Hitler came to power in early 1933 Roth fled Germany permanently, spending the rest of his life living out of hotels in France and other locales in Western Europe. Generally speaking, his life before 1933 was happier than his life post-exile, although use of the word 'happy' to describe Roth might be misleading. Burdened by financial worries and increasingly dependent on alcohol, he became an old man while still in his thirties (a fact he freely and frequently admitted and bemoaned) and died at the age of forty-four in 1939.

Much of Roth's fascinating *oeuvre* has been made available to the English-speaking world only in the past few decades. The last of Roth's completed works were brought back into print in English by Peter Owen in 2010 (*The Antichrist*) and 2011 (*The Hundred Days*). *Perlefter: Die Geschichte eines Burger*, a never-completed novel fragment discovered among Roth's papers decades after his death and first published in German in the 1970s, was until now the only book-length Roth work not available in English. (*Perlefter* is not the only unfinished Roth manuscript discovered and published posthumously; *Der stumme Prophet*, aka *The Silent Prophet*, which he worked on between 1927 and 1929, was not published for the first time until the 1960s.)

Although the incomplete *Perlefter* cannot compare to Roth's greatest masterpieces such as *Job* or *The Radetzky March*, it does offer a glimpse at Roth at the peak of his powers. *Perlefter* is rich in irony and humour. As in many of his best works, *Perlefter* touches upon some of his favourite topics: capitalism, Communism, monarchy, war, revolution and wealth/poverty. Not especially a plot-driven book, *Perlefter* is more of a character study, and Roth does an excellent job painting a portrait of an early-twentieth-century bourgeois man.

A product and representative of the increasingly complex modern upper-middle-class world in which he lives, Alexander Perlefter is an enigma of sorts. He is a brave coward and a wasteful miser; a calculating fool and a vengeful forgiver. He enjoys complaining about how miserable he is, and when he should be happy he seems miserable. What seem to be his most heartfelt emotions are actually just an act. He is ever insecure, easily jealous and eager to please . . . himself. His uncertain eye colour says it all really. His eyes are distinct in their indistinction. They contain little flecks of every imaginable hue. This is a mysterious and indecisive man, one who does not like to commit, an Alexander the Not-so-Great in the narrator Naphtali Kroj's mind.

Kroj himself makes for an interesting character. At times he seems to be almost an omniscient narrator, but his detailed narration is more likely a product of his closeness to the Perlefter family than special powers bestowed upon him by the author. Kroj walks a fine line between neutral narrator and participant character. He lurks behind the scenes for a while and then emerges at the forefront several times – for example, during his scenes with Henriette, his argument with Perlefter on the legal system, his visit to the cobbler and his presence at key events such as Perlefter's flight. These infusions of Kroj are welcome; he may be the most likeable (and level-headed) character in the book. Although the other characters themselves are mostly blind to their own faults and the ironies of their middle-class lives Kroj seems to see through it all, expressing modesty and even disappointment about himself and revealing embarrassment when bringing up sensitive subjects such as Perlefter's secret desires. Kroj's relationship with the Perlefter household is fairly intimate. We must assume that after he arrived as a minor he lived with Perlefter for a few years and forged a bond with each member of the household. Kroj reveals he had been at one time a messenger for Perlefter, that he had played with the Perlefter children and that as an adult he still visited the household regularly. He was trusted enough to have been asked to look in on the vacant house while the family was away.

Of the major players in the book, the one who is least clearly described is Frau Perlefter. We never even learn her first name. Neither do we get a physical description either (aside from 'an awkward girl, no longer young and not pretty'); we get to see her personality mainly through her actions not through the narrator's or Perlefter's description. She seems to be quite weak and prone to outbursts; the only sign we get of her cunning is early on, via flashback, when Kroj mentions that Perlefter 'fathered children against his will'. She lurks in the background through the rest of the book, coming forth to burst into tears once in a while or feel ill. Although Perlefter himself would like to claim the title, Frau Perlefter seems to be the family martyr. It is interesting to note that not long before Roth began writing *Perlefter* his wife began to exhibit the signs of the schizophrenia that would ultimately lead her being institutionalized. It is not inconceivable that some of Frau Perlefter's behaviour is drawn from that which Roth observed in his own wife.

The Perlefter children are comically drawn. They are not given the same detailed consideration as Perlefter himself, but Roth is masterful at accomplishing much in a short space. Each Perlefter child has his or her own particular faults (whether foolishness or vanity or even intelligence), and, although seemingly hopeless at first, each one seems to achieve some measure of maturity and redemption by the close of Chapter VII. Roth devotes the most energy to Fredy, who is a classic wealthy and indifferent bourgeois, as are his friends.

In *Perlefter* affluence leads not to happiness but to insecurity, indecision, dissatisfaction and even boredom. Perlefter desires to marry off his children well, yet when he achieves this dream and his son marries into a very wealthy family under the surface he is actually not happy; he is jealous. Herr Kofritz is *too* rich, *too* influential, and it annoys Perlefter to have to brag about this new in-law. And in what must also be bothersome to Perlefter, Herr Kofritz steals Fredy away by taking the young man into his thriving leather business.

Yes, happiness is elusive for the entire Perlefter clan. The only one who seems happy in the book is Leo Bidak, who does not let anything ruin his mood (Kroj *would* be happy if only he could be with Henriette). Leo Bidak is decidedly *not* bourgeois. He has not achieved that status, not even with his half-house, and his lack of business skills and participation in socialist activities further removes him from bourgeois status. Bidak's ineptitude with money causes him to lose his half of the house. Life has scoffed at Leo Bidak, yet he does not care.

*

In total, the original manuscript of *Perlefter* consists of thirty-two pages. Written in Roth's characteristic tiny handwriting, it is messy in spots, over-inked in some places and faint and faded in other spots. Yet, considering its status as an unfinished work it is surprisingly clean. There are strike-outs of words and phrases here and there and only occasionally whole sentences (in fact, in the entire manuscript of almost 30,000 words there are only twelve instances where Roth crossed out an entire sentence), but never a whole paragraph. Most are isolated incidents except for a couple of places – for example, near the end of Chapter II where Roth had crossed out three sentences but then restored 'He wanted to leave the house' and at the beginning of Chapter IV where he struck out two sentences within close proximity to one another.

Although after reading the entire novel it might seem that the disconnect of Chapter I from the rest of the book might imply that it was actually supposed to be part of some other novel, the page numbering of the manuscript seems consistent with the idea that it was (if not immediately, then eventually) meant to be together with the rest of the book. Chapter I consists of four manuscript pages, half-sized sheets of paper as compared with the rest of the manuscript. The first page is not numbered, but the following two pages are numbered 2 and 3. The final page of Chapter I is not numbered. Chapter II begins on page 4, which would lead one to believe that continuity was intended, although perhaps after some hesitation as to the direction of the novel. *Perlefter* begins in a similar fashion to *Hotel Savoy*, with a seven-storey hotel, but the interesting hotel anecdote is abandoned, standing on its own as a micro-story as the narration moves on to Kroj's situation. Indeed, the first chapter seems to be just a device to get Kroj from his little town into the Perlefter household.

In Roth's manuscript the end of Chapter I is a little choppy. On that unnumbered fourth sheet of paper there is an inch or two of vertical distance between the sentence where Kroj announces that he arrived in Vienna in 1904 and the next sentence beginning 'It was six o'clock . . .' almost as if that were meant to be the opening of a new chapter. At the very end of Chapter I, following the last sentence in the published version – 'Here, one could already hear summer's approach . . .' – there was more in Roth's manuscript, another sentence, part of which was struck out by the author but part of which was not. Roth left four words hanging at the end of the sheet of paper (not printed in the published version), hence the ellipses. It is quite possible, given the choppy state of Chapter I's closing, that it was left unfinished – the fact that Roth in Chapter II says 'As I have already mentioned' when he has not done so seems to bear this out. Certainly Chapter I could have ended with 'On the 28th of April 1904 I arrived in Vienna', but that would create a very abrupt jump into the start of Chapter II: 'I think that now is the time to reveal Perlefter's first name.'

The remainder of Chapter I (the paragraphs that

follow the mention of Kroj's date of arrival) is helpful as a bridge to Chapter II, but it seems not to go far enough. It offers promise, and then it ends. Kroj goes into great detail to describe the sights, sounds and smells of the waking city of Vienna, such that we would assume he will then go on to tell us about his actual arrival at Perlefter's house (which would have been quite interesting), but this descriptive narrative is abandoned, and we rather suddenly launch into Chapter II and a description of Perlefter. Or, more accurately, Chapter I ends and Chapter II does not pick up where the opening chapter left off.

Aside from the questionable Chapter I/Chapter II transition, the continuity of the manuscript from chapters II through VII is well defined. And, although the introduction of Leo Bidak may seem odd, there is no sign within the original manuscript that it was not intended to be part of the story; the page numbers between Chapters VII and VIII are continuous.

There are few concrete chronological clues to work with in the book. The most definite of them is April 1904, when the narrator Kroj arrives at Perlefter's house (or, more precisely, arrives in Vienna), presumably a young teenager at that time (and the only instance in the book when an actual date is given). All other dates are by inference or by reference to a particular event.

The chronology is hard to follow because the narrative in the second chapter remains in 1904 only briefly then flashes back to Perlefter's childhood (presumably around the 1880s) and early career in the late nineteenth century (before Kroj's arrival; in 1904 Kroj already references Perlefter as a rich man established in the timber industry). Rather than an introduction to the entire Perlefter family as it exists in 1904 we get scattered clues (there is a wife, there are four children). Strangely, it is not until Chapter V that we actually learn the names of the Perlefter children. It is as if the narrator Kroj is as obsessed with Perlefter as Perlefter is with himself; only when he has exhausted his description of Perlefter's character and life that we learn more details about the rest of the family; only when he has shipped Perlefter off in an aeroplane do we get a look at the rest of household.

We know that Perlefter has several servants in the household, but not until Chapter V do we learn the name of one, Henriette. Kroj was already at Perlefter's when Henriette began to work for him at the age of eighteen (at one point Kroj references the fact that Henriette was then thirty years old and had arrived twelve years earlier). Kroj was two years younger than Henriette, so he was sixteen when she arrived, most likely not too long after he himself arrived in Vienna.

There are references to Kroj having served in the war and received medals and being taken to the club so Perlefter can show him off, probably around 1919 or so. Perlefter's flight also takes place shortly after the First World War, probably around 1919 or 1920. Logically speaking, if the main action in the second half of the book takes place after Perlefter's flight, 1919 at the earliest, then that would be fifteen years after Kroj's arrival, placing Henriette's arrival twelve years earlier, around 1907, and thus Kroj's age at arrival in Vienna in 1904 to be twelve (if he was sixteen in 1907).

The most glaring chronology issue in the book seems to be centred on Perlefter's flight. When he leaves, the wind from the propeller is described as knocking down the children, which would lead one to believe they are small; the description of a fussy 'young Perlefter boy' refusing to eat eggs and being given chocolate for dinner the evening of the flight seems to indicate the Fredy is a mere child. Similarly, Kroj at one point says of Fredy 'at the time of Perlefter's flight, he was just beginning to grow and be healthy'. However, although Perlefter is supposedly gone for a little over two months, when he returns the children are all seemingly grown and of marriageable age.

Another chronology puzzle surrounds Perlefter's relative Leo Bidak. We are told in Chapter VIII that he arrived from San Francisco with his family at the age of forty-two, having missed the war (and presumably Perlefter's flight as well). Presumably this is during the early 1920s, but the narration immediately flashes back to Bidak's youth in Odessa and carries forward to a time when he and Kroj are friends, which is also presumably before the war. The book ends with the unfinished Chapter X, where Bidak goes to see Perlefter, but we know, based on the narrator's earlier statement, that he has not left Europe for America by this point, so this must have taken place about 1914 or earlier. One puzzling statement, if taken at face value, is the mention of Bidak having lived through 'several earthquakes'. In the early twentieth century, aside from the devastating 1906 quake, the only other one to hit San Francisco occurred in 1911. If we hold Roth to his word, chronologically speaking, that would place Bidak abroad for at least thirteen years, to have survived multiple tremors. Other Bidak-related clues are the fact that he married at twenty-three and then within four years had six children. If it is around 1921 when Bidak arrives from the USA, then it would have been 1902 when he married. The actual last action to take place in the book is Bidak's arrival itself at the beginning of Chapter VIII, about which we know nothing further. What follows is entirely a flashback or recounting of Bidak's early years, in which Perlefter makes only a cursory appearance.

The reader will also note that Kroj's father seems to have met the exact same fate as Bidak's father, a duplication Roth surely would have corrected had he finished the manuscript.

Perlefter is very much a product of its time, both the larger era in which it was written and Roth's personal chronology. By this point in his career he already had enjoyed success as a journalist, completed several novels and enjoyed a growing reputation in the German-speaking world. By 1929 Roth was poised for even greater success, both literary and commercial. For all the flaws inherent in an unfinished manuscript, and despite its relative lack of plot and abrupt ending, *Perlefter* is a remarkable book. Roth paints a number of deliciously ironic characters and, fragment or not, has left us with a work both enjoyable and satisfying to read.

Richard Panchyk
2013

I

My name is Naphtali Kroj.

The city in which I was born is no city at all compared with those in Western Europe. Fifteen hundred people lived there. Among these were a thousand Jewish merchants. A long street connected the station with the cemetery. The train came once a day. The travellers were hop merchants, for our city lay in a hop-growing region. There was a large hotel and a small one. The large one had been built by Wolf Bardach.

His mother was the operator of the steam baths. She died, age fifty-four, from a mysterious disease, a victim of her occupation. Her son, who had studied in the West and who wanted to become a notary, sold the steam baths so he could construct the Hotel Esplanade. He wanted the hotel to look very Western European – yes, even American. To this aim the hotel had to have at least six floors and four hundred rooms.

Futile were the reasonable comments of the many Jews that four hundred strangers would never come to our city. Herr Bardach himself designed the plans. He sent for many men from the great cities of the region. He wore golden pince-nez, a badge of his education, on a silk band. He stood bareheaded, his fat form squeezed into a grey coat, with a stick in his hand when the sun was shining and with an umbrella when it was raining. He had such a sturdy building frame constructed that even with his great weight he could climb upon it without causing it any damage.

As the third storey was completed he noticed that he had no money left.

He sold the property and his plans to the rich Herr Ritz for less than a couple of thousand and, deeply ashamed, set off clandestinely for Vienna to become a notary.

Herr Ritz sent for an engineer, one who sought a great deal of money and was not content with six storeys. He built seven. As the seven storeys were completed the bricklayers in the entire region celebrated. The engineer drank schnapps, walked along the edge of the scaffolding and fell off. His body was so battered that one could not determine whether he was Christian or Jewish. They buried him on the narrow pathway separating the Christian and Jewish cemeteries. Later on the wealthy Herr Ritz purchased him a marble gravestone to compensate.

The hotel was given the name Hotel Esplanade, a name written in gold letters. Herr Zitron from America, whom the people said was a dealer in women, became the hotel manager. It had 450 rooms. But, as the whole world knew that the builder had fallen, no tourists came.

Now back to me. I am the son of a cab driver. There

were twenty-four cabs in our city, one for each hour of the day. My father had cab number 17. To this day I love that number.

My father drove every day to the train station to pick up travellers. He was a strong, bearded man without an education. The only noticeable features of face were the bulbous red nose and the reddish beard. His short brow and his moist blue eyes were shaded by the leather peak of his sports cap. Owing to his profession, he unfortunately drank a great deal. Sometimes when there was no train he had to drive visitors around our area all day long. He stopped at every inn. My father drank schnapps to keep himself warm. Because he was affordable, reliable, brave and able-bodied he had the most customers. He feared neither wolves nor robbers. And the more he travelled, the more he drank. One night, as he returned home without any passengers from a remote inn, his horse and carriage became stuck in a snowdrift, and he passed out immediately.

The next morning he was found frozen to death.

My mother was already long dead. I was glad to inherit the horse and carriage, although I had already learned something, namely reading and writing from Professor Tobias. He was a little old man. When he was young he had a bouncing step. As an old man he walked on tiptoe rather than shuffle along.

Because the homes in our town lacked writing materials he carried ink and quill with him from one student to the next. At home we wrote the lessons with coal from the stove. Professor Tobias was the only man in our town with a top hat. As he had holes in his pockets he needed to wear such a hat. On his head he comfortably hid an inkwell and a feather. This had the disadvantage that he could not offer greetings to anyone. His index finger always rested upon the rim of his hat.

I was, as I said, perfectly happy to become a coachman. But my father's twenty-three colleagues were pleased that he was now in the ground under them. The richest among them, Coachman Manes, bought our horse, our sleigh and our cab. From then on he drove with two horses. He acquired a new whip with a lacquered shaft and a grip of braided straw. On the lash of Coachman Manes were no less than six knots. The whip crackled like a rifle.

Half of the money for the wagon and horse came to me and the other half to the Barkeeper Grzyb, a creditor of my father's. The drivers held a meeting, and it was decided that I should not become a coachman since I had received an education. They said it would be best if I went to stay with my rich relative Perlefter who ran a large timber business in Austria. Rumours circulated that Herr Perlefter was a millionaire. People spoke his name only with awe. The coachmen drank a total of forty-six schnapps one day and gained courage. They sent for Professor Tobias and had him write a letter to my relative Perlefter. The rich Herr Ritz knew the address and gave it to them. The letter was sent, and we awaited an answer. I broke bread every day with one or other of the coachmen.

Winter passed, and as the icicles hanging from the eaves began to melt and the renewing rain began to fall, putting an end to the snow, I became drunk with wanderlust. I was certain that a letter from Perlefter was coming soon.

On one of the first days of March came a brief letter from Herr Perlefter. He would be happy to have me.

I packed for a month. During this time an arrangement was made with Tewje the tobacco smuggler to take me across the border. Easter had already passed by the time the arrangements were finalized. At around the same time my suitcases were ready. On a rainy night I set out from the border with Tewje and five deserters. The customs officer waited until we had vanished, and then out of a sense of duty he fired three times into the air.

On the 28th of April 1904 I arrived in Vienna.

It was six in the morning. The streets of the great city were just awakening. The big ones first and then the small ones. It was as if morning were a family. First the parents awoke and then the children.

Tremendous wagons arrived from the countryside laden with farmers and vegetables. From other wagons came the clinking of milk churns. The houses seemed to me immeasurably high. Behind them the sun was creeping up. It was still chilly. Women with brooms swept their doorsteps. The first streetcars squealed reluctantly on their rails. The conductors rang the bells although the tracks were clear. They clanged out of morning arrogance. The policemen looked on like proud princes. They wore gleaming white gloves. Many of the streets were regal, wide and quiet and clean and guarded by trees. Much was in the air, a rural calm and the slumbering voice of an urban world. The fragrance wafted out of the gardens and into the streets. For the first time in my young life I saw laburnum. I had never read fairy-tales. Nevertheless I knew that these bushes were the fabled trees. Back home there were no laburnum. As I left my city spring had not yet arrived. Back there the snow had just started to melt. Here one could already preceive summer's approach . . .

II

I think that now is the time to reveal Perlefter's first name. He was called Alexander. It is certainly a meaningless coincidence that he was so named – and I don't wish to give in to the seductive urge to make a strong connection with the character and name of my hero – yet I can't help but relate that I lost my respect for Alexander Perlefter for the first time as I recalled how Alexander the Great hewed the Gordian knot with his sword; I imagined that Herr Perlefter had never done anything of the sort. On the contrary. As I have already mentioned, Alexander Perlefter had no love for decisive negotiations or irrevocable resolve. He was not happy entering into those areas from which there were no straight and easy paths back. He liked to linger on the bridges that link one to both here and there because they allowed the person upon them to choose neither. Alexander Perlefter always crossed bridges. He had his cautious nature to thank for all that he achieved. His nature was forged by his own experiences. He was cautious.

Had he been named Florian, Ignatz or Emanuel my respect for him would have lasted longer. He was the first Alexander I had ever known in my young life. To me this name embodied the entirety of Herr Perlefter's personality. But, if I took him for the great Macedonian King Alexander, he naturally failed to measure up by comparison. Yes, as soon as I saw him I had to smile. From the first glance he was unremarkable, just an ordinary man. But when I got a closer look, when I examined the individual parts of his face, his right profile and his left, I knew that there were many secrets that lay hidden within that merited further exploration; I realized, above all, that the name Alexander did not suit him and that such a name as would suit him did not exist. It must be a word, both soft and yet tough, fading away from its own edges into other sounds, indecipherable and thus unusual, of an extraordinary ordinariness. Unfortunately such a name does not exist. Such a word does not exist.

Perlefter's body size was indeterminate. He could seem very small and at the same time very large. If he was unhappy, but also if he was lying, it seemed that he sank into himself like a body made of flaccid rubber. He might sometimes sit on a little children's chair and other times in a large leather armchair. Yes, I find myself in no small amount of embarrassment when I am unable to say whether Herr Perlefter was large, small or medium in size.

He could also, as the situation required, seem either strong or weak, infirm but also mighty. He was able (probably without even realizing it) to change the shape of his stomach, and, as nature had given him a narrow

32

chest and delicate shoulders that gained muscle and fat over time, it remained uncertain whether he was actually broad-shouldered or narrow-framed.

He had a round, balding head and above the neck a small shiny bulge, so that it looked as though his brain could not find a place in its natural shell and therefore made itself a sort of back room. One could not tell at what point the forehead ended and the hair began. The bare skull lent Perlefter's entire personality a rather naked appearance, shiny and needlessly revealing, as if he had bared himself to force your embarrassment. His ears stood very far apart, were small, feminine and could even have been called dainty if had they been pressed closer to the head. They were eavesdroppers, listening to the world from distant outposts.

I could never determine the colour of his eyes. They didn't change – no, they remained ever the same – but they were without colour, rather, a collection of different residues, colours from an old palette that had commingled. Brown, grey, green and amber-yellow at the edges. By day, by night and in the twilight, ever were these eyes so, of an indistinct colour – round, small, open and naked. They were truly the eyes of a difficult-to-comprehend, ever-astonished and good-natured man. They stood very far apart, so that his nose had space to spread, and yet he had been given a narrow, well-shaped girlish nose, slightly flattened at the tip, that glowed like ivory between his round, rose-tinted cheeks. His mouth was also small and his lips red. All the more notable was the space in the middle of his sinuate chin, in which the entire majesty of Perlefter rested and out of which it radiated.

Yes, majesty, for in spite of everything Perlefter possessed a kind of majesty, like most people who are doing well. It was not the majesty of greatness but simply that of well-being. He looked wholly innocent when he was happy, like a chubby child. And yet bitterness slumbered within his joy. And just as he did not like resolute action, he had no resolute sensations. When he was happy, he made himself worried at the same time. As soon as he became depressed he was already hopeful. He could neither love nor hate. He either liked someone or he didn't like someone. Nevertheless he felt apprehensive for his children despite not wanting to. For he feared loss. What he possessed he wanted to keep. He wanted to keep his wife, although she bored him, and he felt for her only what one might for a housekeeper. Men of his type usually loved animals. Perlefter, however, feared animals, large and small; he even tried to get out of the way of birds so they didn't flutter around in front of him. He offered the dutiful cab horses that he encountered in the streets only a shy glance, for he didn't trust a creature he didn't understand. And he treasured the police, not only because they caught thieves, robbers and murderers but also because they were in charge of locking up stray dogs. In the Perlefters' house there were cats, and he would have liked to have shot them had he owned a gun and not been afraid to use it.

34

No, Perlefter did not like animals, and he was indifferent to people. Nevertheless, he was regarded as the most caring family man, the most love-seeking person, the most emotional citizen, for tears came easily for him. He could weep like an actor when the situation demanded it. He could feign joy at the happiness of others. He could play love, hatred, friendship, enmity, excitement, passion, sickness, even intoxication after he had only a sip of alcohol. He did not drink much; he drank very seldom, for he took no pleasure in alcohol. Yet he set out good wine before his guests and claimed to know about it. He tasted it with his tongue when he praised this or that variety, and it was quite easy to believe that he had drunk a lot in his lifetime. Perhaps alcohol would have brought him pleasure if he did not continue to fear that he would lose in drunkenness his composure, his secrets and probably also money. Because of that he had lately begun to excuse himself on account of illness, but he was not sick. But neither was he well. He could become sick if he wanted or when he feared illness.

For even more dear to him than the lives of his children was his own life. In the still of the night hours he could hear Death's approaching gallop. Conjuring fearful imagery, he was threatened by his own imagination. When Herr Perlefter had rheumatic pain in his bones he could already experience an amputation, see a crutch, a wheelchair, an operating table and sharp instruments. And he often had rheumatic pain in his bones and various other pains elsewhere. 'Take care of yourself!' shouted his friends. 'Take care!' cried his wife with fright in her voice, while the voices of his friends quivered with friendly and cheerful sympathy. Perlefter took care of himself, but his anxiety was greater than his care. In the midst of his self-ministrations he was overtaken by fear, and it bore him pain. Because of that his family nagged, 'He's not taking care of himself!'

I should not, at the risk of someone accusing me of injustice, question the possibility that owing to his poor childhood and his earnest efforts he had become somewhat frail. It is quite possible. To tell the truth, Herr Perlefter did have a difficult childhood. He was the son of a poor father of many children who had failed at various careers and whose strict principles could not be loosened by his poverty. Alexander saw himself as the only one among his siblings who could adapt to these strict principles and become the favourite son. By submitting to the cruelty and obeying he deprived it of nourishment. However, the others only increased the fatherly tyranny through their disobedience, poor manners and rebellion against the rules of the house. There was nothing, though, from which Alexander Perlefter was further removed, and hated more, than poor manners. He would not run or climb, he was anxious in front of young ladies – just as he was before the wild boys and teenagers who threatened him – and he told the teacher, the principal and even the caretaker that the others had stolen the bell and put shreds of paper in the headmaster's cap. Alexander brought home the best report card, received some pocket money as a reward and made his way to the circus to see for himself the things of which everyone was so excitedly speaking. He went in a blue suit made of durable rep, with a crisp collar around the neck, and behind him followed his gang of brothers making fun of him. Alexander did not concern himself with them. He knew that they had no money and that they would be turned away at the entrance to the circus. But how did he feel when he saw that some of his brothers infiltrated the line of those who were waiting for tickets to get inside and that they succeeded? Some begged adults to take them in because every adult was allowed to bring one child in for free, and others begged so long that they were able to gather enough money for the entrance fee. Why? Should Alexander give up his precious money for a few horses that were wild anyway and which could gallop out of the arena and into the audience, while the others paid no money for this diversion and thus could truly enjoy the amusement? Alexander was so annoyed that he turned back and informed his father of his brothers' behaviour. For snitching he received permission to wear his new suit of sturdy rep for the rest of the afternoon. His brothers got a thrashing in the evening. He heard them wailing, and each of their cries delighted his heart.

When he was big enough he left school, although a career as a teacher had been predicted for him while he was still resolute in his studies. In reality, nothing interested him less than books and science. Certainly, he would have become a professor if he had been forced

(I know, we've all met this kind of professor), and at wistful times, when Perlefter was feeling nostalgic, he would say, 'If only I had made a sacrifice for my father! What kind of professor would I be now?' Yes, he would have been a professor. What a sacrifice!

But his father was not in favour of him becoming a professor. He sent Alexander to a flour factory. There one had to carry sacks. Alexander did not like hard work. Alexander was so diligent, so mannered, so obedient that he was made overseer of the other sack carriers. Soon he was paying them their weekly wages. Although Alexander was no longer content he enjoyed more honour than his counterparts and was, with little money, a big shot. Other flour handlers took notice of him. But he also had the luck to appeal to grain dealers. He joined a large grain concern. He became the director. He now had a salary and not simply wages. He decided to get married. For a wife is the first step to professional independence – when God provides a dowry the need to earn money is no longer a concern. It was therefore necessary to seek a wealthy wife. He succeeded in finding one. His bride was an awkward girl, no longer young and not pretty. But she was still a girl. She thus belonged to that category of person of whom Alexander was always respectful. He did not need respect in this case. The girl sneaked out to meet him. Out of this relationship emerged a kind of love. It led to a marriage that might be called happy. And as Alexander Perlefter was not very experienced he fathered children against his will. There were four children, and he was now with his brother-in-law's company. It was then that the brother-in-law suffered a fatal heart attack. He left behind a widow. She had always been a little frivolous and to the family was an ill-mannered abomination. Alexander inherited his brother-in-law's business. The widow lost in court. Perlefter paid her every month a small sum of his own volition, as anyone would, he insisted over and over. He said, 'I ask no gratitude!' quite insistently. The widow visited him, she was a white-seamstress, and Perlefter gave her work and recommended customers for her, rich merchants of his acquaintance. For him she took 10 per cent off the price. Perlefter permitted her to demand triple the price from everyone else. 'Herr Hahn can afford it!' he said. But Herr Hahn could also refuse the price. Indeed, he complained to Perlefter about the widow's outrageous requirements, and Perlefter said indignantly, 'Outrageous! I will tell this person!' But the person said to him, 'He's a dirty miser, this Hahn!'

It is quite interesting enough to write in more detail about the career of Herr Perlefter. In any case, it can be seen that, whether good or bad, from the start he had an angel accompany him along his way, one with a weakness for businessmen, removing inconvenient obstacles and associates and diligently rewarding the dedication with which Perlefter saved small or large amounts. For the sake of thoroughness, I will also share that Perlefter was a distinguished businessman, respected member of the stock exchange, that he had begun a wholesale timber business and then had the magnificent idea of using the wood himself. For when he realized, after careful calculation, that those to whom he sold the timber earned more than he did, he decided to be his own customer. He thought first of a furniture business. He could employ one of his countless poor relatives to turn the bad wood into good wardrobes. As it happened, the widow described earlier had married a respectable carpenter. A carpenter who was a relative was certainly better than one who was a stranger. A furniture business was thus not a bad idea. Then the death of another of Herr Perlefter's brothers-in-law brought a still better idea. The brother-in-law died from neglected gallstones and left behind a considerable sum of money and two inexperienced daughters who were not able to make the preparations for their father's burial, and so Herr Perlefter had to take it on himself. He went to a coffin establishment and became annoyed over the high prices. But he was not annoyed for long. As he felt the coffin he realized through his great expertise that it was hewn from miserable wood. One certainly spent more on a coffin than on a piece of furniture. The customers in a furniture shop were young engaged couples. And, from personal experience, Perlefter knew that happiness, particularly the happiness of love, is so overpowering that one forgets to be critical. On the other hand, it could be assumed that misfortune makes one uncritical and blind against the defects of merchandise that was destined anyway to rot in the ground. Who among all the kin would dare to skimp on the last necessity of a deceased loved one? Certainly coffin-making was a brilliant occupation, and the statistics of the previous year showed that there were more deaths than engagements. So Perlefter founded a coffin shop. The carpenter whom the widow had married began to make good coffins out of bad pine. Thus Perlefter was finally relieved of his voluntary commitment to support the seamstress as he had given her husband work.

So Herr Perlefter continued to grow in stature. Among the pillars of human society he was an outstanding one. He could no longer escape the various honours that were bestowed upon him, although he claimed he would have rather avoided them. He became a councillor and member of the Liberal and Moderate Party Club. I cannot underestimate this Moderate Party Club, neither its magnificent facilities nor the integrity and character of its members, their power and possessions. They were men as upright, as solid, as steady as the wide leather armchairs in which they sat, smoking and speaking of the politics of the country and the world. They were council members, parliamentarians, ministers in the making and former ministers. Within the club there were class differences. Naturally Herr Perlefter had to greet a minister first. Naturally the response from the minister was quite condescending. There were moderately educated businessmen and also their academic counterparts, men of scientific backgrounds. This club had numerous tables, and at each one sat a select company. One could determine the influence of a club member by the manner in which they treated the servants, who, like all the servants of the world, were the best at understanding such nuances. And, although Perlefter and people like him were not always pleased with the behaviour of the upper classes, they were proud of this, of their good fortune at being allowed to share the same room with them.

It was, as I said, a club of the Moderate Party, which had no great significance in the country but had newspapers – a lot of papers and skilful pens. It was as if this party had been created for Alexander Perlefter. It was like that bridge where he liked to linger; it required no decisiveness or risky actions – rather, it seemed moderating. It mediated, it created no decisive enemies, it met Perlefter's world view, it left God alone – as well as the princes and the rich people – but also the workers, the homeless and the gypsies.

One might assume that this club was frequented by people such as Perlefter. But it was not so. As far as I could tell, there were not many of the ordinariness of Alexander Perlefter. The opportunity was offered me, on a few occasions, to dine at the club. I came to know some of the members. Perlefter introduced me to them. He did not fail to praise my talents and achievements in front of the men to whom he introduced me, although he himself did not think as much of my talents and achievements as he pretended. Afterwards he did not forget to describe for me, enthusiastically, the importance, the greatness and the character of each man. I recall that neither Herr Perlefter nor I had made any impression upon these people. They nodded in a friendly manner and smiled, revealing their yellowed smoker's teeth and gold fillings, but I disappeared from their memory as might any indifferent object, some insignificant poster or the number of a taxi they had used. I didn't bother trying to make an impression on these great and decorous men because I was too anxious trying to memorize their faces and their mannerisms. Thus I knew that the divorce lawyer, Herr Doctor Sigismund Grunewald, who used to be known as Grünewald, wore a full beard that looked like a black carpet which has become grey around the edges through frequent use. He had rather thin fingers with improbably strong knuckles, which looked like nodes or frostbite scars. With these white and sinister fingers he often stroked his beard, stretching them apart to make a sort of natural comb out of them. At the attorneys' table sat the former minister Lierecke, a man whose bushy beard concealed his upper and lower lip and who liked furtively and absentmindedly to wipe his fingers dry on the end of the tablecloth. There was also in the club the tin-can manufacturer Simmwinger, a grey gentleman with striking and colourful wide neckties and high collars, in whose ears were whitish-yellow tufts of overgrown moss. Frequenting the club was the café owner and former master baker Ringelhardt who owned the three largest cafés in the city and who always spoke loudly as if he were addressing the thousands of customers at one of his packed locations. There also came into the club a pensioner named Major

Grohl, a small man with a red and porous nose who, although he wore civilian clothes, could not manage without the spurs on his boots and who ever lived in an eternal cloud of silver clinking and owned a large sheep-dog that answered to the unusual name of Kratt. There was also the Member of Parliament, Schundeler, a young man from the garment industry who through diligent studies of the national economy and several courses in public speaking had worked his way to becoming a representative of the people. I can recall the tobacco dealer Zopf, the watchmaker and jeweller Beständig, the riding-school owner Nessedolt, the Fire Department inspector Teul, the government commissioner Taklap and the Jewish rabbi Bloch.

All these men esteemed Perlefter. He received respect from all of them. But there were different grades of respect, and they corresponded to the different social levels of gentleman. Herr Perlefter was on familiar terms with some of them. Some he even called his friends. But they were really not all his friends, those whom he thus designated. When he, for example, said 'My friend, the Minister' it wasn't true. It was safe to assume that the Minister never said 'My friend, the merchant Perlefter'. But what did it mean? There was a small nuance. For, in reality, none of these men would have paid him any attention had he not been one of their club mates. They loaned each other money – with interest naturally. They did business with each other but only when each party profited. And thus they ensured not only their own well-being but also secured friendships. For how can one resent an institution that only earns or at least will never cost anything?

Perlefter's membership of this club was seen at home as an honour and a signifier of rank. Frau Perlefter often said to her guests, 'My husband's in a club!' or 'Do you know what happened yesterday? My husband heard it at the club!' She spoke the words slowly, stretching her voice in such a way that the harmless term seemed sinister, terrible, as if it were a supreme court. On the other hand, Alexander spoke of his club as if it were perfectly ordinary and under-standable. 'I'm going to the club!' he said, as one would say, 'I'm going to take the tram.' And so when Perlefter said 'club' there was a moment of silence at the table, and I distinctly believe that each family member was proud during that very brief moment and actually imagining themselves in the club. It was practically as if all the club members were there in the room. It was not as if Herr Perlefter was going to the club but, rather, as if the club had come to Perlefter.

To the family there was nothing that could not be accomplished with the help of the club. 'Enquire about it some time at the club!' said Frau Perlefter. If one needed the assistance of the police, they said, 'Bring it up at the club!' Perlefter himself often said, 'I will see what can be done about it at the club!' or 'I will discuss this at the club!' And only in the most difficult and desperate times did he say, 'I'm going to speak with the editor Philippi.'

The editor Philippi was the final authority and

rightfully so. For he held the post of City Editor at one of the larger papers. Nobody could speak ill of him. He could easily speak ill of everyone else. But he did not often do so. He looked quite dumb but was very intelligent. He had a small, neatly maintained goatee of an uncertain, slightly greenish colour. His gentle large brown eyes were like lacquered lifeless balls. He spoke only when he was addressed. Summer and winter he wore galoshes. Pince-nez dangled from a thin chain over his flowery waistcoat with mother-of-pearl buttons. He liked to sit at the outermost edge of his seat. It was as if he wanted to spare the seat. He was a bachelor. There were rumours that he had had an affair with a housekeeper and had two illegitimate sons. This City Editor was necessarily secretive. One would certainly not like him if one would not need him so often. No, people didn't actually like him, but they did need him often. He had influence. He was Perlefter's most distinguished acquaintance. People often gave him the title 'Editor', but that was not really his actual title, or they pretended not to know that he was not a doctor and called him 'Doctor'. He rejected both. He smiled foolishly with his bulging ball-eyes, but his seeming stupidity was not to be trusted. One said of him that he was a man of honour. He conducted no business. He lived, in reality, very modestly, always wearing his rubber overboots to save his leather boots because in his opinion the streets were too muddy. Have I mentioned this already? He was one of the most distinguished visitors to Perlefter's house. For although to Herr Perlefter education meant as little as poverty, and he held the editor in low esteem because he either did not know how to make use of his connections or had no interest in doing so, he tried to pretend that there was nothing more worthy of respect in the world than an honest and talented poverty, an unfulfilled grandeur. Perlefter casually announced the names of most of his visitors with seeming impatience, almost incidentally. On the other hand, he placed sharp emphasis on the name Philippi. 'Editor Philippi comes today!' said Perlefter. 'He initiated the visit himself.' But that was not true. Perlefter had taken a long time to persuade him. Nevertheless the family believed that Philippi himself had applied to visit Perlefter. And the family was proud.

Professor Strisower was also invited. He was known as the Little Professor. He was an instructor in Oriental languages, a professor for thirty years, hard of hearing, awkward, frail-looking but healthy and untiring. He came, did not recognize anyone, mixed up the children, pondered about common things and accepted the most remarkable without astonishment. One had to peel his coat off, lead him to a chair and make him aware of the food and drink that lay before him. He fastened his serviette tightly around his neck and sat there like a little child and ground his jaws. He listened to what he was told. But he parsimoniously and mistrustfully heard each word that was spoken from across the table. For he was afraid that people were speaking ill of him and mocking him. He was picked up late in the evening by his housekeeper, an evil-looking but good-natured woman with a thick shawl over her arms who waited for the professor in the hall, sitting in the corner like a toilet attendant and slurping tea and munching cakes.

Herr Perlefter sometimes asserted his views about the Professor. 'A poor old man,' said Perlefter. 'He ought to get married. He should have children to provide for him and a wife. For what is the purpose of man on earth? To found a family and to be happy, each according to his options. What does he have from life? And this is a celebrated man, one whom the world has to thank for many discoveries. He is one of those people who will only begin to be appreciated for the first time after his death. I wouldn't like to have his head! What must be going on in the brain of such a man? He must have a hundred thoughts per minute. I have to wonder why learned men aren't better paid. All of them are poor devils!' Thus Perlefter ended his monologue, sorry that he was right.

Sometimes he would suddenly say, and as if a most serious thought had been awakened within him, 'My son will not be a professor!'

No! There was no doubt that Perlefter would not make a professor out of his son. He had great respect for professors, but he regarded them with that timidity which one has in the face of holy men and hermits, people whom one reveres, whom one even holds above oneself, yet whom one deplores and with whom one would not wish to trade places for any amount of money.

He made an exception only for such professors whose knowledge and field of speciality was medicine, the celebrated surgeons who earn thousands with a little knife and whom every man with lung disease requests for a consultation. Two of these famous men were officials in Herr Perlefter's party. But one never saw them at public events; they earned a great deal of money but had so little time.

Among the educated people one had also to consider the great lawyers, whose witty and poignant speeches could be read in the newspapers. These defence lawyers sometimes took on a cause for free if it was a very challenging case and there was a chance they might become celebrities. Unfortunately murderers were not very wealthy. Herr Perlefter felt sorry for the lawyers. 'If I think about it,' he said, 'quite often such a celebrated and gifted man must work for free. And how he must work, the poor fellow! How much intelligence a lawyer must apply! The prosecutor is no dummy either, eh? But the defender must be a thousand times smarter. He can even convince a murderer himself that he has not murdered!'

'So,' I said to Herr Perlefter, 'is that OK? Can one allow a murderer to be acquitted just because the public defender comes up with good excuses?'

'He won't be acquitted!' replied Perlefter.

'But what if he is acquitted after all?'

'It happens once every ten years!'

'That's quite often enough!'

'It's actually very seldom!'

'But let's not argue over this!'

'We already are! I say "seldom"; you say "often"!'

49

And thus could Perlefter silence even a stubborn opponent. He escaped from arguments. He was actually not as dumb as he made himself out to be. It was as if he were made of rubber. He curled himself up, but then he was there again at the forefront, where you had not expected him. The truth was, he actually had nothing against acquitted murderers so long as the defence lawyer gave a handsome argument. These he read at night before he fell asleep in the *Freien Zeit*, the big newspaper that came to the house twice a day and which had a fondness for sentimental and witty articles. Herr Perlefter first read the business section, for which the editor Philippi was responsible. Then came the daily editorial, which Perlefter sometimes read twice. The editorial was always anonymous, but the whole world knew that it was personally written by the publisher of the newspaper, Herr Brandstadt. Nobody called this anonymous personality by name, although everyone knew who it was. One said only 'he'.

'What did he write today in the *Freien Zeit*?' asked Herr Perlefter's brother who never had time to read.

'He wrote an excellent piece on obligations. You must read it!' answered Herr Perlefter.

But when Herr Brandstadt dealt with home politics Perlefter said, 'Phenomenal, this editorial, a magnificent article!' He agreed with all the opinions of the author. Brandstadt wrote to Perlefter's soul. The editor found exactly those words upon which Perlefter had chewed but could not quite get out. Nevertheless it seemed to Perlefter as soon as he had finished reading the article that the very same words had escaped his lips once before. He often said, 'I said exactly the same thing to Hahn yesterday. Today it's in the newspaper.'

What had he said word for word to Hahn? 'On principle, I am against unrest. At a minimum, every incidence of unrest corrupts and damages our business transactions. One mustn't do everything to the extreme. Let me speak of all this. Disputes are unnecessary. One can always reach an agreement. I want peace at any cost. We all want peace. We need it. I'm not in favour of extreme antagonism, but rich and poor must both exist. The rich, however, must sustain the poor. I'll do what I can. God is my witness!'

Well, this was not the speech from the editorial in the *Freien Zeit* verbatim. But the sense was, without question, the same.

Perlefter's political world-view was ever unchanging. Thus the views he held before the war remained the same after the war. Formerly he had proper respect for the Emperor. Although he was not in love with the monarchy, he believed it was a necessity. The war disturbed him, although his earnings were ever greater. Yes, I must confess to Perlefter's credit that he did not like war. It is true that he had been exempted. He had nothing to fear. He feared anyway. Everything was topsy-turvy. If a clerk was absent-minded they could still call him to arms! Out of error, but the misfortune would be the same. When once I came to Perlefter with two medals that had been given to me during the war he brought me to the club. He infused a tenderness into all the words he spoke to me. He led me through all the rooms and showed me to anyone who would see me. He was proud of my bravery, and I had to play the victim that Perlefter was introducing to the public. I played it.

'For what did you receive these medals?' he asked.

'Certainly not for something respectable!' I said.

That offended Perlefter. He was so vain about my medals that my disparagement outraged him. Then he became friendly again.

'Aha, you're modest!' he said.

'No, not at all,' I replied. 'Because it is no merit to be a hero in a war!'

'It is, however, once again wartime,' sighed Perlefter.

And the discussion became pointed once again.

He was anxious about the Russian Revolution. Would they socialize? Would they take everything away from the wealthy like they did in Russia? It proved that the monarchy was the safest bet. If things had gone according to his views they would have left the Emperor alone and yet still made peace. When he saw that nobody was going to socialize anything the Republic pleased him. He preferred not to worry about politics any more.

'Now I have another worry!' he said. But he had no worries.

He bought a large hotel. It was one of the best transactions of his life. But he sighed, 'Ach, this hotel! Why'd I have to buy this? Such a hotel brings nothing but trouble!'

It brought him only money. There was an opening night. His colleagues at the club who had wanted to be ministers had now become ministers. It is true that they no longer had important titles, but they did hold offices whose appellations were still quite lovely-sounding titles. The editor Philippi also came. For weeks this celebration was all that was spoken of in Perlefter's house. Should the children also go? Or Frau Perlefter alone?

Frau Perlefter went there alone. She had a dark and thus youthful-looking evening-dress made for the occasion. She could have wept for joy when she saw the brilliant sign and the dazzling reception.

But she actually wept the next day, for she had lost her brooch in the excitement. 'This is an irreplaceable loss!' said Perlefter. He let his wife cry for the whole day. When he saw that she hadn't prepared any supper he softened, and he bought her a new brooch. None the less the doctor came. Frau Perlefter had a nervous heart. The loss had shaken her. She had to take bromide and yet still could not sleep. Perlefter was sincerely perturbed. He disliked disturbances, disorder, the servants free and running wild, and the commands that his wife issued from her bed made him timid. He wanted to escape the house.

But he didn't leave. For at the depths of his soul lurked the fear of a still worse illness that could befall his wife. He remained at home. He sought comfort in unhappi-ness. 'I'll never get any peace around here!' he lamented happily. Yes, he was genuinely happy when he complained.

III

It happened at this time that the Society for the Advancement of Tourism took note of Perlefter's beneficent work and as a result decided to name him as an honorary member. An honorary member, as you might be aware, has no obligations but many privileges. Perlefter told of this advancement with a sigh. 'This is another thing that will cost me money!' said Perlefter, although it was something that cost no money at all. It was, on the contrary, a thing that brought many conveniences with it. Herr Perlefter received a permanent sleeping-car berth; a place was reserved for the honorary members of the Society for the Advancement of Tourism. Herr Perlefter developed a desire for travel.

He loved changing his whereabouts frequently. He loved to travel. He would have liked to journey to unknown regions had he been able to take risks. Alas, he disliked taking risks, as one already knows from what I have said previously. He never made a journey without being sure that the return would be safe and easy. And he never went without indicating a business necessity as the reason. He was embarrassed, in fact, about the pure pleasure he derived riding the train into the world. Otherwise he would have to admit that travel afforded him pleasure. But he wanted it to seem that he was forced to go.

He wanted to be able to say, 'I have to leave again! Ach, this endless travelling!' It was endearing to him that his family once again asked, with sadness, 'Can't you postpone your travels?' And Perlefter would answer, 'Unfortunately I have to go next week. When don't I have to go? For all I care there should be no railways in the world. To me home is the safest place. Travels only cost money and bring in nothing! One writhes sleeplessly in a strange bed all night long, becomes annoyed about the packing, doles out tips and has no conveniences.'

In truth, however, Perlefter had nowhere so much comfort as in a hotel, even though his tips were not very large. He liked the abundance of warm water and white linen, the breakfast in a great and carpeted hall. He liked the salon music during the afternoon tea and the bustle of the greater world, the mystery of strangers and this atmosphere out of which an adventure could spring at any moment.

An adventure? Was Perlefter an adventurer? Had he not fear of adventures?

I should insert here a general reflection about the complex nature of humans. People can have a very anxious nature and still derive pleasure out of their own anxiety. A man can be cowardly and yet long for situations in which his courage is put to the test. Yes, it is even possible that people long for what they fear. People are very strange.

And if Perlefter was a very ordinary man he was also a very strange man. He wanted, namely, not to be ordinary. He wanted very much to be a hero. He wanted to master each situation, and I know with great certainty that he himself had to suffer most on account of his own cowardice. He himself didn't know how much he suffered. He wanted admiration but had to be content to be pitied.

Was he really waiting for an adventure? Not necessarily! There could be an assault, a theft, a strange note. Perlefter distrusted all the people whom he encountered on his travels. He shuddered when he read about robberies in the newspaper. There were no harmless faces in the world. All faces were masks. Once they fell away murderous grimaces were revealed. Therefore Perlefter was not fond of travelling alone. On the platform he looked for acquaintances. If he found one with the same destination he would be willing to pay them a quarter of his money. A travelling companion received Herr Perlefter's entire affections. He compelled everyone he met on the train to visit his compartment. I, too, have gone with Perlefter.

Perlefter was a nervous traveller. He could not stand it when those sitting across from him looked his way if he did not know them. Therefore he buried his face in his coat. As soon as he entered the car he put on his travel cap, a green-checked travel cap. The top had a button that had become loose and hung crookedly as if dead. Then he buried himself in the newspaper. Only when he travelled did he read the other sections of the journal. Then he became annoyed and looked out the window. Here nature interested him.

Yes, I know you will perhaps not believe me. I assure you, Perlefter was a nature enthusiast. He went into the corridor, pressed his forehead against the windowpane and was wistful when he saw the wide fields, entirely indifferent as to whether they were still bearing ears of corn or whether they had been ploughed. Even snow-covered landscapes made him mournful. In the morning he loved the sunrise, the fog that slowly lifted from below and then quickly dissipated. Perlefter presumably thought of another life when he might have farmed a bit of land. He had a city-dweller's longing for the open country, that of one who wants to be located in the countryside but cannot live without a water closet.

In particular Perlefter could not live without this superior feature of civilization. He had once read of all the various means of contagion, and he feared needing to use public facilities. He avoided them so long as he sat on the train. If, however, he really had to go, it took him half an hour to make all of the necessary preparations. He took soap, hand towel, reading material and eau-de-Cologne with him and went first to check all the bathrooms. He sought the cleanest one for his purposes, and when he returned he looked like a newborn, freshly washed and cheerful and soap-scented, with a new cigar between his pursed lips.

The other passengers caused him great distress. They smoked too much or they opened the window, and that created dangerous draughts which Perlefter asserted had already cost many a traveller's life. Even at home Perlefter monitored the air. 'There's a draught!' he would say abruptly, for he feared the draught, and he imagined that the air was chasing him. Oh, what couldn't come from a draught? A toothache, lumbago, eye inflammation, ringing of the ears, sore throat, lung infection and, when one went to the toilet, stomach flu, intestinal catarrh and diarrhoea. Perlefter was knowledgeable about all diseases, for he felt embattled and surrounded by them; he studied them in order to fight them, avert them and prevent them. He liked to read the encyclopaedia and popular medical brochures.

Sometimes 'something flew into his eye'. It was a cumbersome operation, involving a clean handkerchief, water and a hand mirror. But then followed reservations about the cleanliness of the handkerchief. Perlefter sought solace in a short nap to forget.

That was but a small excitement. The great adventure failed to materialize. Later these little excitements grew in Perlefter's memory into great adventures. Thus he recounted, 'Recently, as I looked out of the window, a large pebble of coal flew into my right eye. Everybody else got off at the next station to search for a doctor. I, however, put myself to sleep, fell asleep, as my eye began to tear up and did not want to stop, and when I awoke the fragment of coal was gone; it had just blown away!'

'How fortunate!' celebrated the family.

There were adventures that Perlefter did not recount to the family. One will immediately know of what type these adventures were when I add that he only spoke about them in the company of men – or, more accurately, gossiped.

I touch here on a topic that is quite complicated, one which I would have liked nothing better than to leave alone were it not so critically important, were it not absolutely indispensable in furthering the knowledge of Perlefter's ordinariness. Yes, I would prefer to leave the whole thing alone. I am embarrassed about the actual and principal adventures of Herr Perlefter, about offering them up to the general public and revealing things that only took place in obscurity. But shame alone does not hinder me. I confess that I cannot assess whether I will succeed in explaining and justifying the adventurous life of my hero, whether it will come across as believable but also generally under- standable. Yes, it remains a mystery even to me where Perlefter got the courage to seek pleasures that truly embodied danger and, worse still, to expose himself to dangers that cost money.

And they did cost money. Perlefter was in no way so tempting that women threw themselves at his feet. No! Perlefter had to pay well above the worth. And therefore it seems to be human nature that the drive for love is stronger than the drive for frugality. Probably even the most timid of men, such as Perlefter, lose any anxiety once the hour has struck for their passion. And certainly a man's virtue is not his most reliable companion. The whole elaborate and painstaking construction that is morality collapses all at once. How simply marvellous the ease with which the pieces can fit together and rise up again.

Perlefter often had moments that one might call weak but which were actually his strongest. Perlefter had a longing for women. By luck, there were women in the world who had a longing for money. And, by luck, Perlefter had money.

I am familiar enough with Perlefter's taste to be able to say that he liked size in a woman: volume and weight. His preference was blondes over brunettes and black-haired women. Perhaps, in fact, definitely, he made no distinction between fake and natural blondeness. No, he could not distinguish fake from natural; he might as well have been colour blind, as he took no notice of make-up and mistook the red of the lips for an abundance of blood and the advanced techniques of love for natural passion.

The reader might ask why Perlefter came to conjure up dangerous situations. But the situations exercised power and force over Alexander Perlefter. He could not resist. He was overcome by the opportunity.

He was overcome by every situation. He loved women but, still more and actually, that which heralds women, that in which they are wrapped. He loved women's clothes. Of women's clothes a specific type. He loved undergarments. Certainly he could not resist any women who appeared before him in underwear. For he could not even resist the magazines on whose covers appeared colour photographs of half-dressed women. This literature accompanied Herr Perlefter on his travels and prepared him for the mood that is necessary for the moral foundations of a man to waver and fall and allow him to fall with it.

In various cities Herr Perlefter knew the addresses of available women who, as masseuses, midwives and beauty-salon owners, came under his consideration. Herr Perlefter noted these addresses cryptically, so that no strangers could decode them, in his leather pocket calendar on the penultimate page, just below the Jewish holidays. In each city Perlefter had a certain hotel, a very specific hairdresser, a very specific passion. He paid gladly but moderately. After all, he had to be willing to invite the lady to a theatre, a concert, a cinema or an opera in order to complete the adventure.

But Perlefter had no interest in public performances of any kind. Everything he saw in the theatre irritated him because it meant nothing to him; he hated the cinema because it was so dark, and he found that he had to pay too much money for the pleasure of watching the agitated shadow-players. Music cut through him like a knife. He became insane with pain. He couldn't even tolerate the harmless but detailed piano-playing of his daughter, even though her teacher insisted that she had talent. Perlefter wanted there to be absolute quiet. Music disturbed his thoughts, his plans for the hours ahead. It weakened his lust, his appetite, all his bodily desires, dazed him and tranquillized his critical thinking. The destinies of others, even if only theatrical representations, were of no importance to him; he was interested only in his own. He worried only about his own fate. There was no room for anything else. Everything else just cost money. With ordinary seats one could not be content. Perlefter had to buy box seats.

But even as great and numerous the pains with which the travelling Perlefter had to contend in purchasing his pleasure, the homecoming Perlefter thought only of the pleasures and no more of the sorrows. The happiness was wrapped in grief that became reduced in his memory like a shell of bittersweet taste around a core that remained more permanently. Perlefter forgot about the expenses, the theatre, the concerts, the operas and the cinema. He recalled only the blonde women and spoke only of them. And although it was practically always the same it seemed to him as if they were ever new, ever chance and mysterious encounters.

'Suddenly', he recounted to a few interested friends in the club, 'who sits down at my table, right up against me, but a large blonde, a curly-haired blonde in a low-cut dress with a dazzling white neck, and of her bust I'd rather not say anything! She orders caviar rolls, and as she eats, I tell you, as she continues to look over at me, I realize how many drinks she's downed. Well, I need not say more.'

Perlefter actually enjoyed his experiences less than the memories of his experiences. As he chewed them over and recounted them he spun a nostalgic gloss around the experiences, of the type one culls from memories and by which they are enrobed, and that was when he first became the bold adventurer, conqueror of women and heartbreaker. As soon as he returned home he delighted in his courage and his deeds. As he conquered his way through his pocket calendar he could already hear himself telling of his conquests, reliving his memories, and it was actually only from his memories that he created adventures. He was like a man who lives for his diary. Perlefter, however, kept no diary.

Yes, he liked to travel. He could not deny, though, that he had to overcome various fears along the way. Although he never admitted it to anyone – and when the occasion arose he freely mocked the superstitions of his wife, the cook and his daughters – he was himself superstitious. He feared a train collision, especially if the porter who took his baggage wore the number thirteen. When Perlefter ascended to his compartment his primary concern was just that there be no collision. Further, he would search with his eyes for the emergency brake. He usually inspected the locomotive before boarding. He knew nothing about the engines of steam trains. Thus he was pleased with the big powerful wheels, the lustrous letters and numbers, the levers, screws and valves, and he sought to fathom whether it was a machine of the latest style or the penultimate one. His investigation of the locomotive reassured him, but he was still far from being certain. Other trains could come, signals and switches could be wrong or the engineer could be drunk. Perlefter prayed silently, quickly, but intensely.

Then something extraordinary happened. As Perlefter was ordering his ticket one day the Society for the Advancement of Tourism explained to him that there was now an opportunity to fly on an aeroplane. Would Herr Perlefter wish to fly? It was a publicity flight and of extraordinary importance, if Perlefter would care to participate. Perlefter said yes immediately. Indeed, he had no idea how he got to the point where his own courage overtook him. A minute later he was so terrified, as if realizing he had just looked Death straight in the eyes. What had he done? Was he a pilot? How did he come to put his life in danger for an organization that did not really concern him? And yet he was afraid to back out. He would become a hero out of fear. I have been told that such was the case for many a hero.

That afternoon I came by looking for Perlefter. It was past four o'clock. He had been expected there by three o'clock. He arrived at five. He was unrecognizable. On his head he wore a brown leather cap. A large green pair of goggles with square lenses lay on his forehead. He came in smiling, into the room in which everyone was sitting at the table drinking chocolate. Everyone stood up, shocked. I had never seen Herr Perlefter like this before.

He sat down at once, talked loudly, ate and drank more than usual and told of his flight.

'I simply must. I can't help it!' he said. 'This is the consequence of honorary appointments. I'll never accept another. But if I turn down such an honour with which mortal danger is associated! It's a publicity flight. Three aeroplanes will take off. I will sit in the first. It is to be hoped that nothing will happen.'

Frau Perlefter began to sob gently. She wanted to call it off. The children did not allow her near the telephone. During the evening they rang up all the near and far relatives of the family and reported to them in detail about Perlefter's undertaking. Frau Perlefter secretly summoned the family doctor to come. Perlefter was still being examined at nine o'clock. The doctor said, 'Not too much to eat and not too little. The heart is fine. Don't look out the window, so that you won't suffer from motion sickness.'

There was a young engineer in the family, a nice young man who understood nothing of aeroplanes as he had interest only in architecture. Nevertheless he was expected to intervene in all technological matters in Perlefter's house. He was forced to repair clocks, electric lights and telephones and to check the drains. Perlefter had, in fact, once helped this young man out. The young man's outstanding virtue was his thanks.

He came over on this occasion. He was given a cup of chocolate. In exchange he gave a lecture on aircraft. He had intended to join the air force during the war. But before he could be trained world peace was achieved. The young man recounted anecdotes of the air officers. It calmed the Perlefter family to see a young man, still alive, healthy and unscathed, drinking chocolate, despite having almost been a pilot.

The family lawyer was also consulted, a walrus-moustached attorney named Dr Nagl who had a fondness for servant girls and thus always entered through the kitchen. He came, explained the airline's liability provisions and advised – cold and heartless as lawyers are prone to be – that a last will and testament be drawn up. Perlefter's wife began to sob once again.

Another relative showed up, one who had not been invited, the poor seamstress who had married her carpenter. She dared not ask the reason for all the excitement. Although everyone else was drinking chocolate she was given tea, and they pretended to look for a lemon. But on this evening the lemons were all gone. She drank it all the same, an old stale tea with beads of glistening foam on the rim of the cup.

They paid no attention to the seamstress. Herr Perlefter lay down on the sofa and smoked. He let his ashes fall lustily on to the carpet, and his wife indulged him. Perhaps, she thought, this would be the last time he could recline so comfortably on the sofa.

Perlefter's thoughts, however, revolved around the immediate future. He envisaged his scattered bones and imagined them being collected and cremated. Perlefter had specified in his will that his remains should be cremated. He was afraid of cemeteries and especially of cemeteries in winter. When he imagined himself as a corpse lying under metres of snow he felt like he was standing outside without a woollen coat. He would rather be burned than to freeze.

Perlefter was also certainly thinking of the hereafter.

For he rose suddenly from the sofa, motioned me in the next room and spoke. 'You could do me a favour. Two weeks ago I heard that the wife of our cousin Kroj is sick with pneumonia. Take this money to him straight away. Have you time?'

'Yes,' I said. 'I have nothing but time to take some money to Kroj. Incidentally, Frau Kroj is perhaps already dead.'

'Impossible!' cried Herr Perlefter. 'To be sure, she's still alive!'

'But what if she's dead?'

'Don't even consider it! She can't be dead! One can't die so easily!'

'Oh yes, one can die easily from pneumonia!'

'Stop it,' yelled Perlefter. 'One shouldn't make jokes about such serious matters.'

Then I took the money to Herr Kroj.

Kroj was a cobbler. The Perlefter family let him resole all their old boots. Herr Perlefter often claimed that Kroj demanded too steep a price and the stranger shoemaker in the neighbouring house was significantly cheaper. Nevertheless all the worn-out shoes found their way to this relative, the cobbler Kroj. It was Kroj's lifelong dream to be able personally to make a pair of shoes for Herr Perlefter. Perlefter, however, covered his needs through the Karlsbad firm of Leiduck and Co.

When I arrived at the cobbler's I could smell vinegar, leather and sweat. Behind a partition lay a groaning Frau Kroj. I rang the shop bell, and Kroj came out in slippers.

'Well, see here,' said Kroj. 'A visitor.'

'How's your wife?' I asked.

'She's already costing me more money than I've got. She's been sick six weeks now!'

'I thought only two weeks? Didn't you write to our cousin Herr Perlefter two weeks ago?'

'No, it's been six weeks since I wrote to him. He hasn't helped me.'

'He's sent you this money!'

'Oh really? He's a fine man!'

Then I returned to Perlefter's. He stood on the balcony of his house awaiting my return. He shouted to me, 'Is she still alive?'

'Yes, she's alive!' I cried back.

When I got inside Perlefter radiated joy. Now he was confident that nothing would happen to him, even if he flew over the ocean in a burning airship. He led me into the parlour. We drank wine, and Perlefter said, 'That's life!'

But we had not spoken at all about life.

The next morning I went to the airfield. Frau Perlefter was there with all the children along with Dr Nagl, the young man who had not become a pilot and the chauffeur, who placed a fur coat in the aeroplane. Frau Perlefter had red eyes. Herr Perlefter stood near the pilot and looked confusingly similar to the pilot. The other passengers arrived in ordinary clothes. They took Perlefter for the pilot and asked, 'Is everything in order?'

Herr Perlefter smiled because he recognized all of

them. The gentlemen had met each other somewhere before. They were all honorary members. They wondered about Perlefter's outfit and asked whether he had flown often previously.

'This is my sixth time,' said Perlefter with conviction.

At ten o'clock the propellers began to spin, and Perlefter's children were thrown to the ground by the wind. The gentlemen climbed in, drew their handkerchiefs and waved. The propellers stopped spinning. Everyone climbed out again. It was embarrassing to both the travellers and their escorts that the aeroplane had not yet taken off. Herr Perlefter kissed his wife once more then gave the chauffeur his hand, for he believed that kindness to others kept one alive. The chauffeur was visibly surprised. Finally the propellers rattled again, and the gentlemen waved conclusively, Perlefter's round face looking out from the window. I will never forget it.

His wife began to sob. She wanted to catch another glimpse of her husband, but he had already ascended to an altitude of three hundred metres. The spectators all craned their necks towards the flying honorary members, but then the large bird vanished behind a red brick wall that restricted their view of the horizon.

Perlefter was flying. Perlefter had flown away.

His family returned home and invited me to lunch 'so it won't be that lonely'. So we sat and ate scrambled eggs, as the roast on this frightful day was burnt. The young Perlefter boy seemed unwilling to eat any scrambled eggs. He was given a chocolate bar, although everyone knew that he had a bad stomach through eating too many sweets. Nevertheless they let him, as I said, eat chocolate.

Late in the night came a telegram: *Landed safely. Your father*. The postman received a tip, and we could hear his joyful footfalls upon the steps.

Herr Perlefter stayed away from his loved ones for more than two months. Let us leave him living abroad for the time being while we dedicate ourselves to his house and family.

IV

I have already mentioned that Perlefter controlled his house. He could control nobody else. Not his friends nor his employees. He could dominate only his family members, for they were even weaker, even more anxious, even more weak-willed than Perlefter himself. They lived in a wealthy household – for he earned and had money – and yet it was a poor household, filled with sighs, worries and bills. The family was convinced that Perlefter was overworked, that he did not sleep, that he was constantly struggling to earn his daily bread, that for him every expense brought new worries. Therefore the family spent not a single penny without concern. There was no joy in this house without underlying grief, no celebrations without pain, no birthdays without illness, no wine without bitterness. One cooked and baked, managed the wash and clothes, furniture, rugs and jewellery, but none of these things in sufficient quantity – on the contrary, it was just the bare minimum, never enough for anything. It was never, ever enough. There was fine cake but cut in such thin slices that one could not taste its quality. Good meat was purchased and chopped into tiny portions. A soup was

71

cooked that would have caused a sensation if only one had the chance actually to taste it. Fourteen guests were invited, but the meal was just enough for twelve. In the ice box were the laughable leftovers, about which one worried as if over the fading life of a dying child. There lay, still and timid, a plate of miserable heaps of butter, yellow and melting into a puddle, awaiting its end. The children's leftovers were rescued from their plates at lunch and the meat chopped up and used to make dinner. Somewhere within closed cabinets dry yellow cake awaited a special occasion. Such an occasion came. It was realized that the cake might endanger the teeth of the guests. Accordingly it was put into the oven to soften, but instead it got charred. It came to the table blackened with a hard carbonized crust. One had to scrape away the crust with a knife. The apples shrank smaller and smaller; they became puckered and the size of cherries. Old oranges grew mouldy and became silvery. The cheapest fruit was purchased. The plums had splits, and their reddish flesh swelled like that of a wounded person. Over the course of time the Emmental lost its moisture and was hard as the wood that Perlefter bought. From twenty different bottles you could gather altogether sixty drops of liquor. In the cigar boxes, which were intended for guests, could be found only one layer of cigars. The curtain ropes were broken for months. One closed the curtains by hand, pulled them together, but they didn't work as desired; they refused. All objects were in a state of permanent opposition. The doors creaked. They had cracks the width of a finger and let the cold air through. Into the large furnace were placed tiny pieces of coal. The humidifier didn't work. The best carpets lay rolled up in the attic, covered with a bunch of newspapers. Torn linoleum was spread on the tables. The pretty red-velvet chairs were covered in white linen, like furniture corpses eerily awaiting their funeral. The flower vases lacked their bases. The coffee service had only nine cups; the tenth was cracked. Near the crystal fruit bowl lay its broken handle. After being worn down through so much use the knives had thin and flexible blades like fencing foils. They were blunt and had to be sharpened daily in the kitchen on the edge of an earthenware pot. The piano was ever out of tune, for Perlefter had bought the cheapest one – one of the oldest – at half price. It was a bargain. The gramophone was hoarse; the records lay worn and dusty in an old cylindrical case. Two pendulum clocks stood, both missing their weights. The alarm clock rang only once a week and only when one was not expecting it, usually after midnight. The doorbell did not work, and on the door was ever the reminder 'Knock loudly!' All the family's umbrellas were broken. The locks on all the suitcases had to be opened by force, because every family member had lost his or her key. There was a clothing stand that could not find its balance and constantly swayed, even if it carried no clothes.

In the drawers of the commode lay the children's still, dead pocket watches next to broken hairpins and dusty yellow tobacco residue. In the inkwells the ink was dry, no more than a black crust. The quills splayed as soon as one put them to paper. There was colourful stationery in all shades; purchased in cheap cigar shops, it was as porous as blotting paper. The postal scale was out of balance. The pencils could not be sharpened, for the lead consisted entirely of fragments and the wood was brittle and fibrous. In the bathroom cold water streamed out of the hot tap and vice versa. The bath towels were frayed. An old mousetrap did not snap shut any more. Inside hung a bait of such a composition that even a hungry rat would be deterred. The laundry cart was missing its right front foot. To steady it a couple of bricks from his son Alfred's set of toy building blocks had been placed underneath. On the mantle stood a plaster ballerina without arms. Under the mirror in the girls' room hung a wreath of pink paper flowers. They didn't throw it out because they felt sorry for it. They liked all broken, defective and useless things. From the proud row of encyclopaedias was missing the volume 'Buddha to Cologne'.

The baker came but three times a week with fresh bread. They preferred to eat it dry and withered, claiming that fresh bread was harmful to the stomach. Old sardines in open cans were refreshed with lemon juice. Marinated herring, however, they ate too soon, before the flavour had soaked in. Breaded cutlets were made that fell apart on the plates. There was cauliflower soup without the cauliflower. Bunches of radishes lay in the kitchen. Only Perlefter himself was allowed to eat them, as long as they were fresh. For only

Perlefter himself lived in affluence. He ate the best soups, the largest and freshest cakes, the specialities, the fresh bread (even though it was harmful); his liquor filled entire bottles; his inkwells were filled to the top with good, flowing blue ink; his pencils lay secure in a shut drawer and were made of the finest material; his bath towel was given to him every morning from the chest (for he would not use the tattered ones); and upon the sofa where he took his afternoon nap there was no white linen. Perlefter was annoyed with his wife's thrift and the miserly disorder in the house, yet was himself the cause of this frugality. For only out of concern about him and out of fear that he might overwork himself in order to provide new things did they keep the old and broken-down furniture and extend their frugality to such things as useless paper garlands. Perlefter, however, did not sigh over the difficult life. His good wife came to the most natural conclusion. Ah! She didn't know that the only reason he came home was because no place else could he find such willing ears that were fine-tuned to his trials and tribulations. He unloaded all his suffering at home and then became annoyed that his house resembled a mortuary.

Outside of the house Perlefter indulged himself in numerous luxuries. At home he absolutely eschewed all delicacies such as chocolates, figs or crystallized fruit. For he wanted to show that he was 'not a pig' and he feared that a father who doles out sweets loses authority over his children. On the way home, however, he happily stopped at the confectioner's and had himself a bite to eat. Sometimes chocolate could be found in his coat pocket in rustling tin foil. This chocolate was usually discovered by his oldest daughter. She came smiling to Perlefter, who then said, 'Oh dear! I meant to bring this to you! I completely forgot about it! Perhaps, come to think of it, I even ate half!' And she didn't doubt his word.

Only his son, who was known as Fredy, enjoyed as many freedoms as Perlefter. Around the time when Perlefter took off in the aeroplane he began to grow and become healthy. When I had arrived he was a cry-baby. Eventually he grew into a mischievous and stupid boy. I really noticed changes as the years passed. Yes, they passed, and Fredy grew. His voice slid into those depths of melancholy descant to which notes of barbarism and sentimentality lend a manly tone. Fredy developed a gradual inclination towards servant girls and in equal measure developed his muscles. He had friends. They came to the house on Saturday afternoons – young men with slicked-back hair in excellent suits with golden bracelets and silk handkerchiefs in their left jacket pockets; young men with smooth faces and abbreviated foreheads. They played whist, they brought liqueur with them, nothing but sweet liqueurs, and amused themselves with confectionary and smoked cigarettes, inhaling each pull with evident pleasure. I never heard them speak of literature. From the pockets of their coats, which were visible in the corridor, protruded colourful magazines dealing with sports, love and 'society'. The young men read fashion magazines. They wanted to look like tailors' models, and they succeeded. It was precisely these young men who set the tone of the city. With a magical swiftness they passed the examination that opened the door to admission into the different universities around the country. Were they not so rich one would have to believe that they were brilliant. Together they joined rowing clubs, they played tennis, they did gymnastics and fencing, some had horses, and they all said they had genuine horseman's legs even if they had, actually, been bowed by a combination of nature and birth into the high life. Each wore a badge in his buttonhole. They were the sons of the Moderate Party and consequently had no political convictions. Young people in bad circumstances are radicals, as they blame the political system for their personal misfortunes. These young men, however, had it so good that to them all political viewpoints were the same. They were thus the future of the Moderate Party. It is an error to believe that the moderate parties of all countries have no future. So long as there are those who can afford the luxury of indifference there will also be moderate people. One might have said that these young men were reasonable enough to remain in the middle. It was actually more like satisfied enough. They were protected on all sides, as they had not severed any ties. They were not strong opponents, nor did they have any.

Such were these young men. Those of them who claimed the spirit fancied themselves to be homosexual, although they liked young girls better. They made off with girls, too, if nobody noticed. As for the young Fredy Perlefter he was still wavering over which sex to choose. But after it became clear to him that he would carry on his father's business he decided upon normal sexual intercourse. It was good to see, as the true nature of the young man gradually broke through. He shed the illness of his childhood days like one outgrows old clothes and in the course of several months became a hero and a sportsman. At the same time his face was also changing, becoming ever more the old, round and slightly girlish face of Perlefter. Fredy's eyes were also colourless and played the events of the world without surprise, wonder, love, compassion or bitterness. With a fearlessness that left him unfazed he plunged into various hazardous sports, and while his family feared for him he won first prize in swimming, track and field and winter sports, and his foolish face graced the illustrated newspapers. I believe that he had no idea he was placing himself voluntarily in the proximity of Death and was not sensible enough to have fear. He had only ambition. He wanted to be the spoiled darling of the family and remain that way, achieving it indirectly by means of heroism. Thus he and his father, in different ways, both arrived at the same goal. Fredy liked to complain about sore muscles. He had 'trained' too hard. He showed several bruises. For weeks he had an arm in a black sling. His mother fed him. One had to hold his jacket and put his socks on for him. After he had definitively decided on the female sex he slept with one of the servant girls and earned himself his first sexually transmitted disease, of which he was quite proud and of which the entire family knew but about which nobody spoke. The servant girl left the house and took a silver service along with her. For weeks this service was the topic of conversation. The oldest daughter maintained that it was silver plate and a wedding gift from Herr Hahn who gave nothing real. Frau Perlefter cried anyway. For her it was silver. To annoy his sister Fredy said that he himself had seen the mark. It was silver. Frau Perlefter's widowed sister, who delighted in the losses of others, confirmed Fredy's assertion.

Fredy loved to recount his various adventures. There was always something happening wherever he found himself. Horses bucked, automobiles crashed into each other, old women were crushed under the wheels, streetcars ran out of power, drunks fought each other, a girl dropped a milk pot. There was nothing too trivial. Everything that happened was worth recounting. Fredy recorded in a notebook the various jokes he had heard. He read some of them out. The others, he said, were unsuitable for women. Nevertheless he was asked to tell them. He recounted them in a low voice, and his sisters acted as if they had not heard. Regardless, they left the room immediately after the punch-line. Fredy rode every morning in the hippodrome. By lunchtime he claimed he could not sit. A gallop had 'upset' him. He drank his soup standing. After the meal he sat down. He had forgotten the galloping. He was regarded within the wide circle of family as a dangerous heart-breaker. He struck up a conversation with young girls in front of the department store. Then he wrote them letters. He showed these missives to his sisters.

'You're not going to believe it!' he said. 'This Margot is from one of the best houses.'

Frau Perlefter was convinced that all the daughters of the bourgeois houses were in love with Fredy. At one point he made the acquaintance of a Hungarian journalist named Roney. Herr Roney was looking for a wealthy man for a singer named Ilona. He found Fredy Perlefter, and all three were satisfied. Ilona didn't like Fredy at all. He didn't love her either. But her name was in the newspapers and on the billboards. The Perlefter family went to films in which she played a supporting role and to the cabarets in which she sang. Ilona was not so young any more. Her picture stood on Fredy's writing-table along with a couple of letters written in large stiff strokes on pale purple paper. The letters lay there, casually strewn across his desk, and his sisters secretly read them. Fredy came home and said bitterly, 'You've already read my letters!' but was actually pleased.

Since Fredy 'had something' with Ilona, he entered into those wonderful circles where art blends with sin and justifies it. Behind the scenes it was quite different. Outside the boundaries of middle-class society much was not only permitted but also desirable. 'Art' legitimizes even debauchery. Through his relationships within the arts Fredy put the whole family into an adventurous mood. Fredy used up half of Frau

Perlefter's spending money. He wore, henceforth, silk shirts and gave his opinion on his sisters' clothing. He must have known what attracted those women living in that world in which the main thing was the effect, the effect about which people would gossip. Frau Perlefter and her daughters were far removed from wishing to be such a woman as Ilona. But to be mistaken for an Ilona in certain circumstances was the dream of the Perlefter girls. There came a free spirit to their clothes, a new rhythm in their lives; their appearance received a fantastic boost; they let each other tell jokes without embarrassment any more and spoke with frank gestures of truths which for girls of good families should be but fairy-tales.

Yes, with the entry of this Ilona into Fredy's life a lot changed. One even spoke about his long and torturous sexually transmitted disease, and Frau Perlefter, feeling left out, asked Fredy all kinds of discrete details. The boy had to invent them in order to avoid losing his reputation. He had made love to Ilona three times and endured her and her friends for three months. The letters stopped. He began speaking to young girls again, and as he had already indulged in the realm of the arts he no longer wrote to girls who were the daughters of wealthy citizens but, rather, to the denizens of the theatre world. Within the family, however, reverence and awe for the first in the series of artists, Fräulein Ilona, were preserved. Quite often a family member came across her name in the newspaper, spoke her name aloud, and distant relatives who were reliant upon Perlefter's good will came to tell that they had heard and read of Ilona's latest ventures.

Fredy didn't cry over her. She had given him what he needed: calm at home and validation of his reputation as a seducer. He went to the summer resorts and the winter spas and received innocent postcards from his sports partners. The family took each harmless greeting as a clandestine confession of love. Fredy's actual affairs were with hotel chambermaids and a generally available widow whom he considered the great love of his life. The Perlefters had no anxiety that their son would forget himself and marry a pretty woman without any money. They knew him, the family, and they trusted in the power of the blood.

And it truly seemed that Fredy was letting his eyes roam over the daughters of the land in order to locate love and a dowry to defray its cost. It was clear to him that he must have an attractive wife. Although she should have money she should also be generally pleasing to men. There existed this type of girl in the world, and Fredy courted them. He spoke with them about respectable things. He read a couple of books to acquire potential topics of conversation, and he believed that I could be a valued guide for him in these matters. I recommended history books to Fredy, for I believed that the best way to impress educated women was by spouting forth dates. I had no experience with educated young women. But I soon learned from Fredy that they were bored by historical dates. I picked up a book on art history and recommended a conversation about paintings. These women didn't go to museums on their own. I resorted to natural history. Fredy read the chapter in which the piquant processes of the science of procreation and reproduction are detailed and was henceforth no longer reluctant to discuss natural history. And he would have luck with it, for he soon began to court a young girl whose father owned a majority stake in the Hinke Beer Brewery. It seemed that Fredy's scientific references made an impression on the girl. Fredy was invited 'to the house'. He brought a bouquet of flowers, and he went by automobile. I have never in my life seen a bouquet like that. It was expensive, discrete and exotic, and yet it was still winter. Who knew from what garden these flowers had come? Perhaps they cemented the relationship.

Everyone awaited Perlefter's return. A celebratory atmosphere spread through the house as if in anticipation of joyous events. Fredy received no more letters. Suddenly he had grown and was ready to become engaged. While I squandered my formative years with useless thoughts, he grew into mature adolescence and positioned himself into a profitable marriage. He was a splendid boy, and he fulfilled his destiny in an exemplary fashion and to everyone's satisfaction.

V

Unfortunately Fredy's engagement could not be officially celebrated. You see, one had to consider his sister, who was older than he. And, as far as anyone knew there was not a suitor in sight.

It was a shame. The eldest had already dispensed with men. She was, unfortunately, named Karoline, and that troubled her and paralysed her courage before men. Although known as Line in the family that also irritated her. She had once been pretty; to me she'd once been very pretty. Oh, as I arrived at Perlefter's she still wore her hair in a ponytail and swayed her hips when she walked. Her hair was brown, hard, crackling and unruly. She was very arrogant, little Karoline. She was a character. She didn't cry; or, more accurately, at least not when anyone could hear her, for her small grey malevolent eyes were often red. She was the wisest and most taciturn member of the family. She was always sitting with books and always achieved the best grades and was rarely sick. Back when I still played with the children she tormented me the least. She isolated herself from me, and there was always some invisible fence around her. She read the most books and always placed one on her lap when she came to the table and hastily gulped down each bite so she could return to reading. At night it was her light that burned the longest.

But it seems that the education of a young girl can damage her charms. For, although Karoline had reached that age when she was not yet quite marriageable but at the point when an interest in men should have awoken within her, it proved that she had absolutely no interest either in her own appearance or in men. Indeed Karoline wore her crackling, unruly, provocative hair smooth and brushed back, and as a result one saw that she had a high, pale, arched mathematical brow and small, pretty earlobes whose delicacy was lost in consideration of this significant forehead. Every young man grew afraid of this head. Every man had to take this girl seriously and consequently could not fall in love with her.

Karoline studied mathematics and physics and was an assistant in some scientific institute. There she put on her heelless sandals, a blue work uniform, took a manly umbrella in her hand and in her wide breast pocket were jingling keys and a glasses case of black cardboard. Karoline was converted into a doctor.

The family praised her delicate ears and her hair, which to them and others were more consoling than the scientific standing of their daughter. But soon even the family succumbed to the allure that seems to surround laboratories and assistants, and everyone admired the achievements of such a young child.

'She should have a husband,' said Frau Perlefter.

Karoline became angry when one spoke of her. She rushed out of the room and slammed the door shut; the walls shook, and from behind the door one could hear sobbing.

It was customary in the Perlefter family that everyone kissed one another. Only Karoline kissed nobody. At great celebrations, at farewells and birthdays, she blew cool fleeting kisses from indifferent cheeks.

She had cold dry hands with pale, flat fingers. Her fingers looked like rules.

A husband was sought for her.

Sometimes Tante Kempen came; she had already dealt with many girls in the family. Tante Kempen had large brown shining eyes that seemed to absorb everything but in reality were practically blind. Glasses had been prescribed which, out of vanity, she spurned.

She knew all the suitable families, this Tante Kempen. Every week she was invited to a different house. She was like a wandering spider, spinning her web from one corner of the city to another or like a wind distributing fruit seeds around the world.

Tante Kempen had identified a man for Karoline. He was a lecturer who needed money in order to become a professor without worries, a scholar, a pleasant, forgetful young man. But Karoline was terrified of scholars.

The Perlefter family didn't know what to do. Frau Kempen began to consider the other daughters. In any case, Karoline went her own way, and I will get to this later when the occasion arises.

Frau Kempen focused on the second child, who was called Julie. She was gentle, pale, anaemic, and she drank Chinese wine and swallowed iron pills that caused chronic constipation. The doctor ordered her to take walks, but to do so Julie would need comfortable sandals of the type her sister Karoline wore.

Julie wore vain high heels and small patent-leather boots that caused her pain. She liked to buy fabric, colourful scraps of lace which she stored in the drawer of her chest. What she liked most was to lie on a cold bed and sort remnants of silk. She had four seamstresses, for new and old clothes, for both alterations and 'modernization'. All the men liked Julie, and she left the selection up to Tante Kempen.

Herr Perlefter, who was ever practical, wanted to have an engineer in the family but not the type who could design bridges. Herr Perlefter wanted a practical building engineer who could appraise a house. During this time there were many inexpensive homes being constructed, but each appraisal cost 'a fortune'. And yet engineers earned so little. Perlefter wanted to have a handyman in the house.

Frau Kempen searched frantically and could find only an architect with artistic ambitions.

But he had a studio. He gave parties. One spoke of his reckless life, and a report from the Argus Detective Agency revealed that he had considerable debt. The worst was that his family was unknown, that he was 'alone in the world'. Argus could not discover the profession of his father.

'Perhaps', said Herr Perlefter, 'his father was a bartender or a pimp or a brothel owner. Who knows? The apple doesn't fall far from the tree!'

It was quite hopeless. Frau Kempen could not even get the Perlefters to invite this young man over 'without obligation'. She thus turned her attention to the third daughter without the second being completely removed from her thoughts.

The third daughter was the most prettily named, Margarete, and she deserved this apellation. She was lovely. Yes, I liked her. Had custom not demanded that an errand boy not fall in love with his employer's daughter I would certainly have fallen in love with Margarete, but back then I was still a messenger for Perlefter. Later I saw that it was a good thing I did not give my heart to Margarete. You see, she was an unhappy person.

She was unlike the rest of her family; light and cheerful in disposition, she let nothing come to confrontation. One took her for an obedient and authority-respecting child. She kissed everyone who offered a cheek for her to kiss. Generally speaking, it was believed that she could tolerate anyone.

By the time she was fourteen years old many young men were in love with her. But around then she loved her history teacher. At that time she also had the best grades in history. The next year she loved her literature teacher and forgot everything about history. She learned to play the piano but was quite unmusical.

She trilled melodies loudly and tunelessly all morning long.

Later she met a young socialist and gave herself with ardour to the party secretary. Every Sunday she went in wooden sandals into the forest with the workers' children. She taught the children to sing, and all of them sang off-key, too.

Under the influence of another young man, who gave lectures at the community college, she immersed herself in Steiner and Nietzsche. She understood not a word of either. But she was proud that she was so cultivated.

When someone told her that it was abominable for a woman to be idle she applied for a job as a stenographer in a bank. Over ten poor candidates who needed the job Margarete was victorious. For she was Perlefter's daughter. She even received bonuses while the other girls were dismissed.

Margarete was pale and thin, and she could not stand the air in the office or the typewriter. Thus she gave the position up and became a kindergarten teacher without pay. But she understood nothing about kindergarten, and they dispensed with her assistance.

After that she arranged charity balls, surrendering herself to the duties of a committee member.

Next she dreamed of having a salon with poets, artists and scholars. Her husband should not play a role in this venture but should have money.

Frau Kempen went in search of such a man.

Eventually she found one.

In the meantime, however, something important happened in the Perlefter household. All other things of importance faded into the background before one particular event: Henriette got married. Henriette was thirty years old and had been with the household for twelve years. I remember how she looked when she arrived. She came direct from the country, eighteen years old with red crackling hair, and she smelled of laundry soap bars. One could hear her stiff under-garments rustling.

I loved her.

She was the product of a random adventure when the police sergeant connected with her mother eighteen years earlier as he patrolled his route alone. Her mother brought hens, eggs, bread and radishes into the city.

I went once with Henriette to her village. She wore a hat with glass cherries and held her shoes and stockings in her hand, since the road was muddy. We walked through the fields, the crickets chirping and the glass cherries clinking. Henriette told me all sorts of things that Perlefter's wife and the porter's wife said – for example, that Henriette would be better off in a position with a childless couple. But Henriette feared her mother. Under another employer she might perhaps go astray. It seemed to me it was Henriette herself who was most afraid she would go astray.

She was red and flushed, and we were both hot. Then Henriette took off her hat, and it seemed to me that her hair was fragrant. Yes, it smelled very much like hay, meadows and dew. We stood still, and the wind caressed us. It was late spring, and one could already hear summer's gallop.

Then Henriette told me that a new constable had arrived in the village when she was fourteen years old. He had been a handsome officer, fearless and with shiny buttons. So, I thought, Henriette loves a policeman.

But in the course of the conversation it turned out that this constable was a pretty despicable fellow. He had seduced three fourteen-year-old girls, taken their cash and disappeared.

I don't know whether Henriette was one of those fourteen-year-olds. But I am practically convinced of it.

In the woods a solitary bird was warbling, and we argued about its type. I was two years younger than Henriette, yet she debated with me as if I had been the same age as she. She was the only person who had respect for me. I was a man.

I said it was a goldfinch. Henriette suggested an oriole.

I began to quarrel with her. But even though it really was an oriole and Henriette was right, I did not yield.

Finally she hit me, and I pushed her back, but I bumped into her soft breast, and my anger dissipated. I protested no longer and smiled as Henriette threw me to the ground and pounced on me.

We lay together in the woods, the wind was warm and fresh, and the oriole warbled. And we got carried away.

I was determined to marry her, but she cheated on me with a chimney-sweep, yet loved me still. The older

I got the more she loved me. When I took leave of Perlefter she kissed me, and sometimes she came to me 'just for a quick hello'.

Henriette could not marry the chimney-sweep, for she could not let go of the Perlefter family. She had announced her intentions and was already making preparations for the wedding. Then Frau Perlefter became sick. She had a weak heart. So Henriette stayed.

After that she chased after a man from the gas works. He even came into the kitchen on Sundays. But the reason for this was a suddenly flaring love for the two maids.

After that a policeman, a tailor and a mason came on to the scene. All of them wanted to marry Henriette. But she hesitated for quite a while, for she could not leave Perlefter's house. The policeman died of pleurisy, the tailor disappeared from the picture and the mason fell off a table in his house and broke a leg. It was quite remarkable that the mason fell off a table despite having the chance to plunge from respectably high scaffolding on a daily basis. He made a fool of himself and fell off a table. Perhaps he had, at that moment, been thinking of Henriette. Henriette visited him once in the hospital, but she could not tolerate the smell of iodoform. She fainted and never returned.

Yet I knew she would come to me if I were bandaged and reeking of iodoform in the hospital. For Henriette had not forgotten me. She loved me more maternally, and the older I got the younger I appeared in her eyes.

I accompanied her more often to her native village. I carried her hat and, when it was wet, also her shoes and stockings. Once when her mother was sick, a second time when her stepfather died and a third when her uncle married his third wife. But we argued no more over the species of twittering birds. We consistently agreed about all things. We spoke about all our concerns, and sometimes I even related something from books I had read. Henriette was very proud of me and prophesized a great future.

We abstained but loved each other none the less.

I would have done anything for Henriette. But we didn't use the familiar form of 'you' in front of others.

She suggested that I should turn my attention to Margarete.

I then had much money. Surely I was worth much more than those young men who came to the house.

'I don't need money,' I said.

'You're a foolish boy!' said Henriette.

So we walked peaceably next to each other and arrived at the village. I ate cheese and sour milk and porridge that Henriette cooked for me. Porridge was usually eaten only by the sick and by new mothers. Before I went to sleep Henriette squeezed my hand.

It was just around that time, when Fredy's engagement party was to take place and when Perlefter had returned home from his bold flight, that a rich and widowed farmer courted Henriette.

When Perlefter heard about it, he said, 'We cannot and must not stand in the way of their happiness!' Frau Perlefter began to cry. She even began to feel ill and took bromide. But this time Henriette stuck by her decision to marry. She was attracted by the large farm and the role she would play in her village.

It was ambition.

The Perlefter family decided that Henriette could go off immediately after Fredy's official engagement.

But Fredy's official engagement depended on the engagement of his sister. Henriette, meanwhile, worked on sewing her trousseau. Every Sunday she went to the village. She brought back milk, butter, radishes, sauerkraut and country bread.

She looked almost like her mother did many years before. One had to look at Henriette's face for a long time to realize that she was once pretty.

By this time Henriette had a pale yellow face. Neither the joy of surprise, nor heat from the kitchen, nor a winter's storm and wind could turn her cheeks red. They were emaciated cheeks. Her forehead jutted out and shaded her face, and deep within, like bay windows, lay her triangular-shaped blue, pale and hard-looking eyes.

And yet I still loved Henriette, and every day I was ready to marry her just as she was with her strong bony hands and skin that was like leather.

When Perlefter found out about my love he took me for crazy. He was speechless.

Perlefter was already two weeks at home. But he was still recounting stories of his travels. If one should believe him he had journeyed across the entire world. Yes, he was even rich in new artistic impressions. He had visited museums and studied paintings.

He appreciated only the dimensions of a painting. Perlefter liked to say, 'Colossal! Such a painting!' He was actually only describing its size. His highest praise was 'As large as the wall!'

He sought to discover how long the painter of such a work had worked on it. Since returning home from his travels he read the art news for two hours a day. One time he went to an auction. He brought back to the house a painting of a dark-green sea on which a boat with two sailors rocked. He hung the painting in the salon and showed it to all his guests. 'When I'm weary,' he said, 'I place a chair in front of the painting, sit myself down and study it. I could look at it for hours. This is art!'

Meanwhile, his daughter Karoline, the one they called Line, was annoyed. Yes, she was bold and said, 'You don't understand anything, Father!' Then Frau Perlefter began to weep. She could not tolerate it when someone was offended.

But Perlefter didn't concern himself with his daughter's criticism. He regarded her as the least worthy of his children. 'If someone has studied,' said Perlefter, quite correctly, 'one knows what one wants. God knows what will come of this Line! Frau Kempen hasn't been around?'

Exactly! Frau Kempen came after a few days. As a precaution she had a list with her, but with her glassy and blind eyes she could not decipher a single name and refused to wear glasses. Herr Perlefter took the list from her hand and read, 'Albert Koch, officer of Goldlust and Co., thirty-five years old; John Mitterwald, born in

America, very rich; Alex Warjuschin, from Moscow, fled from the Bolsheviks.'

Perlefter interrupted the list and said reproachfully, 'Nothing but strangers! Nobody knows who their parents are! If I'm going to give my child to someone I must know who, what and how he is!'

'First we should hear more!' urged Frau Perlefter, for she was afraid that Frau Kempen would be offended.

But Frau Kempen once again knew nothing of the parents.

'Come with very precise information,' said Herr Perlefter. 'You need to treat this like a business. If someone offers me something . . .' At this point Perlefter broke off. He was embarrassed to admit that he looked at his sons-in-law from a business perspective.

However, Karoline had proceeded with a significant change. She dressed herself carefully, she wore flowers on her chest and flowers stood ever in her room in various drinking glasses that had disappeared from their normal place in the household. I watched as Line blossomed and was young again, and once I ran into her on the outskirts of the city where there was a decent railway station but also pretty meadows. She sat on a bench with a young man. She rose and asked me not to mention this.

'Naturally!' I said.

Then something surprising happened. Karoline gave me a kiss. Oh! If only she had given me this kiss when she still wore a braid and swayed her hips.

The young man was a poor chemist. He had one arm in a sling and had shoddy boots and a battered hat. He was certain he wanted to be an inventor. So Karoline went her own way. I later learned that they had a small apartment, Karoline and the young man. One day I was invited over to celebrate the birthday of the young man (his name was Rudolf). We sat, the three of us, and drank and ate moderate but festive things. A purple silk tie lay on the table wrapped in thin paper. Karoline had purchased it. Karoline and Rudolf kissed constantly. Rudolf had injuries on all his fingers – he was quite diligent in his experiments. He wanted to marry as soon as he succeeded with his invention.

But, after three months passed and still no success, Karoline took the household by surprise one peaceful evening, while everyone was shelling nuts and said, 'I'm engaged to be married!'

A great confusion arose. Herr Perlefter pulled himself together first and said, 'One shouldn't make bad jokes about serious matters.' Then Karoline started to cry, and it was the first time in her life that she wept like that, such that everyone could see and hear her.

Perlefter let a long time of pleading pass before he consented. For a few days there was a mournful air in the Perlefter house, as if someone had suddenly been snatched away from them.

Perlefter took the occasion of this mood to eat at the club. After a few days he said to Karoline, 'Bring the young man!' It was as if he had ordered her to bring him a nutcracker.

Ultimately, a poor chemist was better than nothing. Now Fredy's engagement could also be officially announced. The young chemist was very depressed when in the family circles. He bowed to everyone and sat stiffly at the table like a schoolboy at his desk.

Nobody knew who his parents were either. Perlefter said to all his friends, 'A quiet young man! He will certainly be a great inventor. One can also earn a lot with inventions.'

Thus Fredy's engagement was celebrated, and the young chemist got a couple of new suits. The wounds on his fingers finally healed and did not reappear. Had he decided not to invent any more?

One party chased the other.

After some weeks it was Henriette's turn. I accompanied her once again and this time had a heavy suitcase to carry. Henriette sobbed the whole way. I attended her wedding. I gave her a gramophone and was held in high esteem.

'He's like my own son!' said Henriette.

I danced with her, and then we went outside to cool off. Henriette said, 'When the old man dies, you'll be my heir!'

The old man, however, will live until Judgement Day. He is hardy, taciturn, and his face looks like it was hewn from the brown earth. He is never angry, never friendly, always alert; his tiny little eyes are forever wide open as if they have no lids and never require sleep.

Henriette is a brave wife, and she waits in vain for his death.

VI

Herr Perlefter had much to sigh about in those days. The demands of his wife and his engaged children escalated. Herr Perlefter revelled in complaining. It sickened him a bit that the family no longer had time to deal with him. From the delightful centre, in which he had lived year after year, highly visible, respected and pitied, he had slipped more and more to the periphery. His son, his daughter and his son-in-law lived like distinguished guests in his house, and there were days when lunch was served without waiting for Perlefter, even though he was only five minutes late. When he arrived the family said they had assumed he would be at the club that day.

The family took up irritating habits. The old order was no longer maintained. Once Henriette had left the house the maids changed quickly, and Perlefter could tolerate no new faces or new names. He called all the girls Henriette – whether their names were Anna, Klementine or Susanne. Usually their name was Anna.

One prepared for the 'quiet weddings'. Invitation lists were assembled. The household trembled with joyful agitation. 'We're getting old!' said Perlefter.

He feared age. He thought about his father who had lived to the age of ninety-two and become a revered burden to his children, even an obstacle. Perlefter did not wish to live that long. He would have completely given in to this miserable mood had his son's party not compensated for all the trouble through which he had to suffer for the celebration. It was a magnificent party that Fredy threw, so much so that one could even forget about the poor chemist whom the inept Karoline – and it had taken long enough – had selected.

It was a magnificent party. Alexander Perlefter could not have wished for a better one. Fredy had married into one of the richest families: his father-in-law was the leather-goods manufacturer Kofritz, the same Kofritz from whom all the pocket mirrors, fashion accessories, sport jackets, dog muzzles, horse saddles and travel-manicure sets originated; the same Kofritz who produced the best leather armchairs in the world, wonderful seats and recliners that were customized to the size of their users, whether wide or thin, short, average height or tall. It was the very same Kofritz whose initials could be seen on the most distinguished luggage of the most distinguished travellers, whose crest was a lion pelt with the printed motto 'Respect the Trademark'. Herr Leopold Kofritz was a self-made man, just like Herr Perlefter. But in the most important things these two wealthy men were different from each other. Above all, it was how they spent their money. If one could say that earning money is a talent, so one could say with even more certainty that spending money requires a certain character. In this regard, I should note that knowing both fathers well Perlefter had only talent, while Kofritz also had character.

Leopold Kofritz was known as a 'generous businessman'. He did not seek to elicit compassion from those around him as Perlefter did but, rather, envy and admiration. He didn't wish to be loved but feared. He didn't want to win over his fellow men he wanted to amaze them. He was more brutal and less fearful in nature but by no means decisive. His hesitation always wore the mask of determination. When he still didn't know what he wanted after a long time it seemed to others that he knew for certain. One said of him that from the first moment of his career he knew that he would produce the best leather goods in central Europe. He liked to tell of his beginnings, and he assured all those who believed him anyway that even as an errand boy in the steel industry he already had a great interest in suitcases. If one heard him speak this way one had to believe that the true merchants and manufacturers, those with very particular talents for their specific industries, were blessed by God Himself, just as was the case for sculptors, painters and musicians. One had no doubt that the young Friedrich Kofritz had an inner voice calling him to the great showcases of the leather industry. Fate had chosen him to produce leather goods under a trademark that was, in truth, not original but ingenious.

He was small in stature, tough, broad-shouldered, with a low forehead and thick, stiff black hair. Although he was of minimal body size he filled the room with his personality. He did not demand absolute silence as Perlefter did. One could even contradict him. He countered each argument with his healthy smile, his strong white teeth, his blood-filled red lips and his twinkling, squinting eyes. Although he was never actually right he upheld his side using the casualness of the mighty, who require no logic because they have power. Unlike Herr Perlefter Herr Kofritz made no small excuses. He said only 'So! Do they?' and in this question lay the entire scorn of an expert against a dilettante. There was no area in which Herr Kofritz had not achieved mastery. It seemed that he had been through everything. But he had no experience, nor did he require any experience to be heard and respected. He had the best and most indisputable tools to back up all his assertions: health and wealth. In the society circles frequented by Perlefter, Herr Kofritz was the richest. He maintained the best relationships. He was so powerful that he did not need to search the club to see in which room his chairs and sofas were. Yes, it was as if he was wielding his influence over the highest authorities in the country through his seating. Not even ministerial seating was treated with such importance.

Herr Kofritz was an impressive man in every way. He had much more money than Perlefter. He had a large house, a lot of servants, a business automobile and a luxury car, two handsome dogs; he went hunting and even knew how to shoot; he associated with high officials and radical monarchists, and he was himself not averse to the idea of a monarchy. He did not fear authorities as did Perlefter; rather, he loved them as one loved his peers. Herr Kofritz had ten titles and twenty honorary offices; his worth multiplied, his property was ever greater, his factories grew and his workers never went hungry. Although his father was only a moderately wealthy Russian Jew who had emigrated, Herr Kofritz had the demeanour, voice, inflexion, manners, confidence and ideology of a long-established, firmly planted conservative. Although he belonged to the Society to Combat Anti-Semitism he was also part of the Society Against Eastern European Jews. He chose the Central Party and declared himself, if one asked him, in favour of their political aims. But what he enjoyed most was amusing himself in the Conservatives' Bowling Club, and he gave as many donations for national purposes as he did to the fund for war veterans of the Republic. He gave to both sides with the same determination. Nobody could reproach him for anything. He was one of those public benefactors who occupy an outstanding place on the list of professional scroungers and among charitable ladies. His name was in all the newspapers, in all stories about donations received. He once told Perlefter that he had even had an office specially built just for charitable purposes, which was tasked with managing public collections in the newspapers and handling applications. Herr Perlefter spoke some days of this office.

It seemed to me that Herr Kofritz was in agreement with his daughter's choice. He wanted to bring Fredy 'into the business'. First, Fredy had to become a capable horse rider. He rode every morning through all the avenues, so that anyone near by could locate him. Frau Perlefter allowed herself out of the house once to see her son ride. Fredy also liked to go out in the afternoon in his equestrian outfit. He wore a bright-white tie, and the family said that he looked like nobility. Herr Kofritz gave him a horse. On the saddle were the initials and the trademark. Fredy's whip had no equal in the entire riding world. This whip was new and yet as worn as that of an old equestrian. The handle was an owl's head with amber eyes. A wonderful leather loop wagged below it like a dog's tail.

If one studied the sporting magazines and pictures one learned that every refined rider has a refined dog to follow along. Fredy obeyed this rule. To the great terror of his father he purchased a wolfhound that was quite tame but who Fredy claimed was quite wild and vicious. I have never in my life seen such a kind, gentle and trusting dog. But the entire family trembled over his terrible ferocity. The whole family was amazed at Fredy, who placed his hand between the animal's sharp white teeth. Fredy seemed to be a lion tamer.

Perlefter said, 'I don't want any dogs in the house.'

So a kennel was built for this silent animal, who crept through life like a pious martyr; a kennel meant for the yard but which was usually left in the hallway, where it lay near the coat rack as if guarding this apparatus.

But if Perlefter had to enter the hall he said, 'Fredy, take the dog outside!'

And just as one feared the dog one marvelled at the

wife. Everything about this woman was wonderful. First of all her name – she was called Tilly. Fredy called her Till. Her hair was dark blonde. The family called it a 'coppery sheen'. Tilly had long teeth and short lips; her exposed gums could be seen when she smiled: 'A unique dentition, teeth like pearls.' Tilly was slim with a clear tendency to be broad in the hips. The family prophesized eternal slenderness for her. When she smiled one praised her eternal cheerfulness. If she was melancholy one admired her mature seriousness. If she quarrelled with Fredy they were charmed by her temperament. When they flirted one spoke of her 'maternal disposition'. Even Fredy's sisters, with the exception of Karoline who was occupied with her chemist, were in love with Tilly. They now went to the tailor who sewed for Tilly. They let her give them the address of new dressmakers. Perlefter's youngest daughter gave up all scientific and social goals. She returned to the tradition of her sex, worried no more about unmarried mothers, no longer read the society magazines that were delivered to the house every week and neglected all charity balls. Margarete was as pretty in those days as when she was eighteen years old.

The good influence of the Kofritz house on that of Perlefter was unmistakable. Henriette had to experience it! She had to experience how the porter-woman now gave the rancid butter to the cats instead of using it for Sunday's biscuits. But Henriette was now a rich farmer's wife, and her husband would not die.

The connection of the two houses was a beneficial

relationship for each. It turned out that the manufacture of leather goods could benefit from the help of chemistry, and Karoline's chemist obtained a position. This fact reconciled him with the world he had always treated sullenly and shyly. He was talkative, and a talent awoke in him to tell anecdotes. 'The young fellow is a good businessman!' said Perlefter. The chemist could also perform various exciting card tricks and other magic. Since he had not injured his hands any further he was quick, and before they were aware of it the copper coins were hidden in his coat sleeve.

Why should he not also enjoy the comforts of life? He had been poor for so long, and this poverty, which had so many disadvantages, compensates its favourites by bestowing upon them a certain earnestness, even if they don't deserve it. Some people look important just because they are poor, and one is inclined to ascribe genius to a pauper when in reality it is only misery. The great unjustness of the world order tempts us to attribute greater value to the poor, even though poverty alone should be reason enough to love those afflicted by it. Karoline's poor chemist (his name was Rudolf) looked, with his wounded hands, so genial that I thought he would, tomorrow or the next day, invent a new gunpowder. As soon as he slipped into his first good suit he developed a banal social talent, and a couple of weeks later he was employed in a leather factory. I imagine he was not bad. Perhaps he had actually invented a superfluous gunpowder.

The Kofritz family lived in a suburb where no dust

could penetrate, in a district from which germs were banished. In front of the house was a small ornamental garden and in the back a large orchard in which the birds from the whole neighbourhood gathered to twitter. The terrace looked out over this great green garden, and Perlefter was invited one afternoon to take tea there. He complained of a headache. He could not tolerate the twittering of the birds. He praised his own house because it didn't have a terrace and asked, half indignantly and half sympathetically, 'What did Kofritz build a terrace for?'

There were a few little things that Herr Perlefter didn't like. I think, if I may say so, that he sought to retaliate for having to endure singing the praises of Herr Kofritz for several hours a day in front of strangers and acquaintances. Therefore, Alexander Perlefter looked for flaws; the larger the better. That Kofritz spent so much money annoyed him. He criticized the fact that Fredy had to ride instead of 'looking after business'. But no one except his poor wife now cared for his advice and his foul moods. He stayed ever longer in the club where he was appreciated because of his new family ties. He allowed himself to celebrate, and yet I believe that it brought him no joy when one appeared to celebrate him while actually celebrating Kofritz.

Tante Kempen came to get her commission.

'This marriage was truly made in Heaven!' said Perlefter and cast a glance at the ceiling.

Frau Perlefter cried, for she could not tolerate any quarrels, and she hurried to give Frau Kempen some costly pineapples. Tante Kempen ate pineapples as if this magnificent fruit was an ordinary apple. She was indignant. She even said, 'This marriage is far from complete. It is first an engagement!'

At this point Perlefter grabbed his chequebook and paid Frau Kempen her commission. In exchange she had to forgo pineapples, and instead she got cherries, which at that time were just beginning to ripen.

Frau Kempen placed little value on pineapples. She was not offended; she wanted only to garner for herself an invitation from Kofritz, and she succeeded. Herr Kofritz had a poor niece who lived with him whom he wanted to marry off, and he could use Frau Kempen's services.

Frau Kempen even knew an appropriate man, a young journalist who worked for a large publishing house and who was waiting for the death of the local editor to be able to get married. By luck the young man, named Hirsch, got himself into the film section of the newspaper and received a salary increase.

I met the young man at Perlefter's. Herr Hirsch had a substantial physiognomy and, despite his youth, little hair. Frau Perlefter made the apt but somewhat general observation that the young man looked 'like an actor'. He had short legs and a long thick torso. His rigid nose sprang out with imperious confidence.

This young man was considered by the family to be a 'gifted writer'. He sometimes brought free tickets. Herr Perlefter thought highly of him, although he still earned little. Unfortunately, Julie Perlefter was once again bedridden. Even before she had a chance to recover her health the young Herr Hirsch had decided upon the Kofritz niece. It seemed to me that later, after Julie had recovered, Herr Hirsch was sorry that he had been so impatient. He had chosen for life and could not alter his decision.

He soon married and became head of the film section. Had he taken Perlefter's daughter he would certainly have moved into the commercial section, to the columns in which the important writers develop an interest in the stock market.

Fräulein Julie was now expected to be healthy for a half a year, and Frau Kempen made use of this time. She knew a dentist without a practice who had a great desire to establish himself.

He was a handsome young man with girlish pink cheeks and bright-blue eyes and a short moustache. He liked to tell 'jokes for gentlemen' and amused Herr Perlefter away in a corner.

Enquiries were made into his past life, and it was learned that he had a mistress.

Herr Perlefter had nothing against a mistress, whom one could easily discard. Furthermore, he was sympathetic to the idea of a dentist in the family. How often did one or another family member have a toothache? The dentistry bills always accumulated at the end of the year.

In general Herr Perlefter was in favour of a practical son-in-law, as I have mentioned once before. Everything that was a danger, a pain or an evil should be immediately averted. He longed for a solicitor for his youngest daughter. By surrounding himself and his family with a protective force of experts he believed that he could not only protect his family but also save money.

Unfortunately, Julie's health did not hold up as had been predicted six months earlier. She had an abscess, a hateful and downright proletarian illness and, moreover, on a place on her body about which one could not speak easily, a location one could divine based on the silence it inspired.

Consequently, Julie could not lie on her back, and thus the bed no longer gave her any comfort. She was operated upon twice. The family doctor came twice a day, and the surgeon came three times a week. When her bandages were removed Julie was emaciated, and as it was not yet summertime it was decided to seek a health resort for her.

Herr Perlefter, whose digestion was not very good, would enter a spa for stomach ailments. He had to drink water and exercise. In contrast, his wife needed complete tranquillity, for she was nervous.

Karoline and her chemist sought a serene place, such a location in which one could experience the most idyllic existence. Fredy was to go with the Kofritz family on a little trip through Europe and then stay in Switzerland where there were mountains for tourists and valleys for automobile tours.

The youngest daughter, Margarete, was to accompany her mother, although it would be very boring. Frau

Perlefter could not travel alone. She knew nothing of the outside world. She did not understand train schedules, she was shy and even fearful, and it was impossible for her to sleep alone in a hotel room.

Thus remained Julie, who did not want to go with her mother since Margarete would be there. The abscess had interrupted the handsome dentist's courtship, and he had to be given the opportunity to continue in a summer resort. That could spell trouble for Margarete, since she was more beautiful and healthier. It was predicted that even in a health resort Julie would seek a bed. In that case, the invited dentist would accompany Margarete, and one knew that the walk around the health resort was lonely and in the evenings so poorly lit that she might be seduced into imprudent activities.

There were therefore many difficult problems to resolve within the Perlefter household, and they even asked my advice, although I was a novice in such matters. None the less I suggested that the dentist only be invited when Julie had fully recovered her health. He was invited for a week, and in the meantime Margarete was sent to be with her father at the spa.

In mid-July the Perlefter family was scattered in various recreation spots, and I often went to visit them by train, bearing bunches of flowers.

I was asked to take a peek at the Perlefter house from time to time. I promised I would do so. I was told that the silver utensils were stored in the wood-burning stove in the salon.

The alpaca cups stood in the linen closet. On the

floor lay the rug, rolled up. The lamps were covered with large white sacks. The windows were bare as in sick rooms; the curtains lay in the laundry room. It smelled of camphor to combat moths, and every evening the cook played the gramophone.

That summer I went to live with Henriette in the village, and I was pleased to see how capable she was. Her husband feared her. She slapped the servants, and she boxed the maids. All was tidy on this farm. The watchdog loved Henriette and stayed at her feet. Sometimes she slaughtered the chickens herself – with a sharp knife she struck a confident blow – and then I got a good soup. She didn't let me get up before eight in the morning, and after sundown she told me that the farmer had at most a year to live.

Henriette was still pretty, at any rate it seemed that way to me, and I confess that I was not certain whether she also appeared so pretty to others. Back then I wanted to become a farmer, who sowed, ploughed and harvested and never wrote a word.

When I returned to the city there was a letter waiting for me. Fredy had married *en route*; the celebration would be held later. Karoline had also married the chemist. The dentist was on the verge of becoming engaged to Julie. Frau Perlefter had no more headaches. Herr Perlefter's digestion was in perfect order. Margarete danced diligently and yet gained weight. Overall the weather was beautiful. It hardly rained that summer. Such a dry summer is apt to put the wealthy into a good mood.

VII

A half a year later – it was winter, the time of year for balls and dressmakers – Margarete got engaged to a gentleman in the prime of his life, a man who made table lamps. His lamps were of a very special type, made from a material that looked like porcelain and yet never broke, decorated with colourful ornamentation which could never fade, with movable shades whose position could be adjusted. The most important thing about these lamps, however, was the fact that the inside contained one or more little bulbs, so that a faint, mild, milky light streamed out, the room darkened and yet illuminated, the most excellent lighting for people who suffer from insomnia, who fear the dark or who are disturbed by an ordinary lamp. A light that was also useful in salons in which intimate societies sat, for lovers who no longer need to see each other but do not want complete darkness and for ageing and ill-looking women whose fading looks are still beautiful if a dim and colourful shadow is cast upon them.

One should never draw conclusions about a person's character based on his profession. In this case, however, I cannot deny a correlation between the gentle light of the table lamps and the lyrical soul of Herr Sedan, as Margarete's fiancé was called. The historical name had no bearing in this case. When one saw Herr Sedan one thought not of history. He looked fat and mild, and he possessed the gentle softness and warm goodness of a man whose soul was well cushioned and protected against any attack like a well-padded suitcase. Across the wide bridge of his nose sat his ancient black pince-nez with thick, sharply polished glasses that slightly shrunk his large eyeballs without robbing them of their lustre of goodness. Herr Sedan wore dark suits that made him look slim, obscured his belly and mellowed the girlish red of his cheeks. He was someone who wrote no poetry, yet one could still say that he was poetic, so I call him a poet, a passive poet. And even this restrictive attribution loosens when I consider that the lamps of the Sedan factory were actually poetry.

One must remember that Margarete's goal was to operate a salon in which true artists could convene. Consequently, her fiancé began to finance an artistic magazine. He located a man of letters, a writer of feuilletons who had long been seeking funding. His name was Dr Feld, and he wrote under an Italian pseudonym about fashion, art exhibitions, social events and also about women. This last them e he handled in the form of aphorisms that he scattered in various magazines, as a farmer spreads seeds over the fields. One read the aphorisms there where the sketches left off and the advertisements began, brief lines punctuated with dashes on smooth shiny paper in a delicate font, and the reader sensed immediately a man of mind and world. Herr Dr Feld now brought a new magazine into existence. It was richly endowed and appeared irregularly, not because it lacked money but, rather, because its publisher and creator considered irregularity a quintessential characteristic of refinement.

All the wealthy members of the family and their distant relatives subscribed to this magazine. It had a somewhat obscure name. It was called *The Blue Margin*, and I guessed that Herr Dr Feld himself had devised the name. Many collaborators spent their Wednesday afternoons at Frau Margarete Sedan's. She wore wondrous clothes and gained a little weight. She met all sorts. A young lecturer in history was recommended to her. He came and gave lectures on Napoleon to a small group. Within the circle that surrounded Margarete Russia was in vogue. Margarete began to learn Russian. Her teacher was a refugee Russian engineer with no papers and no money. He liked to speak of the cruelty of the Bolsheviks, and one could tell that he had lived through it. He favoured all people who were upset by revolutions. It was quite agreeable to please these people, because it was they who had money. The engineer gave Russian lessons to many women. He was a small agile man with a bald head and deep little watery eyes. Margarete said there was something demonic about him. Herr Sedan spoke with him about electricity. Occasionally the engineer switched to business. He had dealings with the film industry, and he sold equipment on commission. He rejected nothing. He accepted everything that came across his path. For a time he ran the publicity for a Russian cabaret. In the winter he accompanied the Sedan family to Switzerland. In the winter's calm of a health resort, in the face of the majestic mountains, something must have happened that induced Herr Sedan to decide to divorce Margarete. The engineer found other students. Margarete returned to Perlefter's house.

So there she was. Frau Perlefter cried for three weeks. Margarete came to the divorce proceedings in chaste high-necked clothes. Her lawyer said, 'Lovely.' In the evening Tante Kempen arrived with a new suggestion. Herr Perlefter was going to a sanatorium in an effort to recover. He would give some thought to a new son-in-law later. But scarcely a day before his departure Margarete brought a bank official to the house whom everyone liked because he was so modest. Perlefter postponed his travels. Two weeks later Margarete married her bank official. Herr Perlefter took him into business. Suddenly Dr Feld was back. He began to opine from within the pages of *The Blue Margin*. Margarete promised to provide the means. He bought her jewellery, and a week later the whole world could see her picture in *The Blue Margin*. The Wednesday afternoon gatherings lived once more.

Margarete was fat again. As soon as she married she grew, and nothing could help her. Every morning she did gymnastics. A masseur was recommended, a noted masseur who served the most distinguished houses in the city and commanded the highest prices. He was a handsome muscular man in leather leggings with a wide mouth and white healthy teeth. The bank official was jealous, but it was no use. He played no role at all in the household. When Margarete was in a good mood she stretched out her hand to him. He had to kiss it. When he wanted to speak she interrupted him. Eventually he began to brew tea, tend to the hearth, fetch water and run to the pharmacy. He wanted to be useful. He recounted to patient listeners school stories and anecdotes about life on the stock exchange. He was, unfortunately, a bad storyteller, and from his first sentence one could already predict the end of his story. Dr Feld despised him. Dr Feld was practically as revered as the masseur. Margarete confessed her sorrows to him. The bank official was dumb enough to defend the accuracy of the scales. He wanted to prove that the masseur was superfluous, but he demonstrated only his own expendability.

So passed the months. Perlefter was in the sanatorium. His wife lived with Fredy, whose wife was going to have a child. Karoline also bore a girl. The chemist took her out for a walk. He was a good father and no longer felt a need to invent gunpowder. He pushed the pram, lived outside in the austerity of the countryside and demonstrated a genuine interest in leatherwear.

VIII

While Herr Perlefter was in the sanatorium, recovering from the calamities that had afflicted his house, there landed on one of the European coasts Leo Bidak with his wife and six children along with his entire fortune, which one could fit in a straw basket and still have room to spare. I knew Leo Bidak from my childhood and from my home town. He was related to Alexander Perlefter, who granted no special significance to this family link. Leo Bidak came from San Francisco. He had survived several earthquakes and had missed the European world war. He left to earn money, but he returned as a beggar, and he once again sought 'a reason for existence' after having had to give up several existences on both sides of the ocean.

He was forty-two years old, a family man, and he had experienced much and learned nothing. He'd had a few different jobs, and not one of them had he mastered to perfection. In his youth he had been a longshoreman in Odessa. Back then he could still break thick paving stones on his knee and balance a Cossack sabre on his fingertip, crack a hazelnut between his fingers and uproot young trees with one hand. He was so strong that he was compelled to demonstrate his prowess, and since dock work did not strain him enough he supplemented it through fights in saloons and quiet alleys. On Sundays he appeared as a wrestler in a circus and followed the rules just as minimally as the laws of the country, which he despised, because he was one of those unusual people for whom the state was a stupid institution that robs liberty. Consequently Leo Bidak had not only the authorities for enemies but also professional associations, and as he had never belonged to the Association of Athletes he was considered in the sports world to be a querulous outsider who won all the prize competitions without paying any contributions, enjoying all the privileges without subjecting himself to the obligations. In addition, Bidak was a favourite of the crowd, who had no qualms when he made a mistake and forgave all his illegal moves while others who did the same were booed out of the arena. And so Leo Bidak had to fend for himself, a rebel within his own profession, unclassifiable in any category or species, lonely and mighty, averse to society and his own confederates, against both worlds. He was short and fat; his hands were round and soft with short fingers like those of a child, and yet his grip was firm. These hands were like iron when they were clenched into fists. I once saw Bidak's palms and was amazed at their clear and simple lines, the likes of which I have never encountered in anyone else. There were three heavy furrows, two lateral creases and a long line. Everything else was smooth, like a palm of sanded skin. According to the rules of palmistry Bidak had at least 150 years to live, without sickness, without pain, without complications. His hands were tools; when he wasn't working or hitting they hung there limp from his strong round wrists like a pair of hammers.

Even his face was simple. It consisted of a low forehead, tiny blue eyes, a short nose, a small but wide chin and two strong cheeks, on whose surface muscles could be seen flexing. Behind the forehead lived the simplest of minds: the eyes had nothing else to do except look out for danger; the nose needed only to smell, the mouth only to eat. Even Leo Bidak's hair was only there to meet the requirements of nature. It had no colour. It was neither thick nor thin, neither hard nor soft, and Bidak wore it as God let it grow, falling down over his forehead or cut very short, depending on whether or not he had money to go to a barber.

For Bidak had no money, and he earned only a little. The wages he made at the circus he drank and gambled away. Three dice of human bone rattled constantly in his right trouser pocket. He won at games only when he was drunk; he lost when he was sober, and that is why he never came into money, because he spent whatever he had. He lost on the street whatever else he put up – paper, watches, a pencil, smooth pebbles, keys and tools. He needed the stones to practise marksmanship. He had such skill with slingshots that he could hit a specific windowpane on a moving train. On free afternoons he went out into the fields through which the train crossed, lay down in the grass and made a mental note when he heard a train coming to hit the third or fourth or fifth windowpane of the third to last car. He always hit it. That behind the windowpane people sat he knew. That he might unknowingly hit one delighted him much. Sometimes he flew a kite made out of newspaper. He carried a ball of hard dark-blue twine in his pocket, twine that he, with his small, wide and sharp teeth he could chew through and with which he could sew his clothes and also his boots.

For a time he was a driver for a distillery, and the smell of alcohol dazed him so much that he became drunk without drinking. He knew how to deal with horses, for his father had been a driver, owner of a wagon and two white horses, of which one died in its youth and the other reached an advanced age and after the death of old Bidak was able to serve three more masters. The elder Bidak drank heavily and froze to death one winter on the road, in a ditch into which both horse and carriage had fallen. He left his son an old house, a barn and a large Rosskopf clock that could go for three days without winding. Horse, wagon and sleigh were bought by the bearded Coachman Manes, who, now with two horses, experienced an unexpected windfall, gaining many customers and procuring a new whip with a handle of hard leather and a six-knotted leash. Bidak did not like the driver Manes. Leo went to his mother's relatives in Russia and was a worker in a port instead of what he would have been entitled to: horse, wagon, sleigh and customers and a new whip to crack.

As driver for the distillery Leo one day fell asleep in

his seat, drunk from the alcohol fumes; the horse became frightened, a child got under its hooves and Bidak was fired. He joined a sugar and tea wholesaler and was charged with unloading and stacking the large black-packaged sugar loaves. He learned a great trick: he could carry half a hundredweight at once thanks to a contraption that he himself had invented, a small wooden stairway with three steps that hung on his back and carried ten sugarloaves on each step. A wrestler came to visit him at work once, and Bidak hit him in the head with an entire load of sugar. The athlete was dead on the spot.

This murder happened in the gloomy hallway that connected the offices of the trading house with the warehouse, at a time when only a hard-of-hearing senior accountant was still present. He had heard neither the quarrel nor the fall of the sugar and the wrestler. Bidak dragged the dead man to an adjacent property, pocketed his belt as a souvenir and buried the body. Then he returned to work. The senior accountant had missed him and called for him, and because he had not come Leo Bidak was dismissed. A week later there was a story in the sports pages about the sudden death of the wrestler. At that point Leo Bidak made his way to the West.

In Perlefter's city lived Bidak's aunt, named Frida Sammet. She owned a laundry and pressing establishment, which she herself operated. Her husband, who was able to write the occasional verse of poetry, had a gentle nature and was abused and subjugated by his wife. He was a silent and witty man with no job but with many talents. He once wanted to be a writer, and he had even already published a work, a book for shy young men on writing love letters which found many readers and buyers. Herr Sammet was in favour of practical themes. He wrote a pamphlet about foot-and-mouth disease, about the souls of dogs and a protest against compulsory vaccination. He occupied himself with the occult, hypnosis, eye care; he owned a microscope and a furnace; he believed in a perpetual-motion machine and in alchemy, and he often read the encyclopaedia and foreign dictionaries. He did not allow himself to miss a single foreign word, pursued each to its origins, and in this way came to a disorderly but extensive knowledge. His wife was at times very proud of her educated husband, especially when she spoke to strangers. At home she scolded him and forced him to perform humiliating chores. At ten o'clock he had to be lying in bed, at seven in the morning arisen; he was not allowed to drink any alcohol, could smoke only three cigarettes a day, could not eat cured meats, nor herring, nor onions, nor fresh bread, nor roasted potatoes – all the treats for which Herr Sammet longed. He hated his wife – which would surprise nobody. The hatred connected them as a chain binds two inmates. Nevertheless they developed similar faces over the years. Both had narrow, withered cheeks. The difference was that Herr Sammet's mouth was a friendly curve. Frau Sammet's mouth, however, was like a long, narrow and greatly faded brush stroke. Her voice was sharp and thin like a sword. Herr Sammet's voice was imperceptible. He always spoke silently, like someone who has lost his vocal cords.

Day and night he mused about taking revenge on his wife. He owned the house in which they lived and in which the laundry was located. He kept a few hundred gold coins in a secret compartment. It was the last bastion that he successfully defended against his wife. He spoke often, happily and almost frivolously, about his death. For he did not fear death in the first place; rather, he was looking forward to the hereafter, a subject in which he was very well versed, and to his existence as a spirit which he believed he had secured. Secondly, he knew that he had nothing more to expect from life and that the iron-clad health of his wife would continue for a long time. He could enjoy actual pleasure only when dead. This joy was in part based on his the confidence that Frida would not find the gold coins. But he did not even begrudge her the house. By law it would go to her at his death if he did not give away it during his lifetime. But he had no friends and no sympathetic acquaintances. Then Leo Bidak appeared.

He arrived just on that fateful day on which Frau Frida Sammet had put her left arm through a windowpane and severed an artery. Herr Sammet, who had mastered the art of healing, knew that it was of critical importance to stop the bleeding and to bring the arm into an extended vertical position. Because he was creative he laid his wife out on a table, constricted the arm above the wrist with a handkerchief, took down the lamp hanging from the ceiling and connected, by means of a rope, the extended arm to the hook on the ceiling. Thus, helplessly bound, lay Frau Frida in the middle of the room when her nephew Bidak arrived. In this position she could not offer him a warm reception.

Bidak entered the business. He helped the girls by ironing and starching the laundry; he sorted the shirt collars and the stiff shirt breasts and freed white curtains of their yellow rust stains. He brought the clean clothes to the homes of the better customers and invoices and warning letters to the defaulting debtors. Frau Frida Sammet had reason to be pleased with him had dissatisfaction not been her nature. She was thus unhappy with her nephew. She complained about him to Herr Sammet. But he took Bidak's side. Frau Sammet complained about her husband to Bidak. Then she learned, to her horror, that her nephew and her husband were friends.

Yes, they were friends.

Herr Sammet spoke with Bidak about all profound questions that weigh upon mankind. They went for walks together, watched sunsets, noted wind direction and stargazed on clear nights. They also talked politics. Leo Bidak was just as dissatisfied with the world order as was Herr Sammet. They were both unhappy.

They were determined to reform the world. Frau Sammet forbade her husband from attending socialist meetings. She could not forbid her nephew. To irritate her he wore a red tie, and he even came to work with a red carnation in his buttonhole, and on May Day he let the pressers have the day off. Frau Sammet would have fired him long ago, but she could not. The older she became the greater the number of clients who were in arrears. Perhaps Leo Bidak was a revolutionary spirit, but he could not be called unreliable. He had great strength, and on busy Saturdays he mastered over a thousand stiff dickeys. At six o'clock he put the work down. For sorting the laundry he demanded a premium. He was, without question, a radical socialist.

After a year, he knew Herr Sammet's secret hiding place for the gold coins. Then he asked for a raise. Frau Frida hoped to learn the secret from him. She increased Bidak's salary, but she learned nothing.

'The money lies behind the painting with the black ship,' said Leo Bidak. But it was not there. 'He's hidden it again,' said Bidak.

At one point Herr Sammet fell ill. He had a notary come and gave Leo Bidak half of the house.

Herr Sammet regained his health. But he was not sorry that he had given Leo Bidak half of his house.

Now Bidak had a half of a house. He was already twenty-three years old. At this age men normally begin to look for a wife. Bidak fell in love with a girl named Ellen who had learned shorthand and was a socialist.

Leo Bidak and Ellen met often, they read books, and Herr Sammet was pleased about these young lovers.

One day Leo told his girlfriend that he had killed a wrestler. He told her only because he loved her ardently and trusted her.

But Fräulein Ellen could not bear the thought that she should kiss a man who was a murderer.

For three weeks Ellen avoided her beloved, and Leo fell into depression.

Then he went to see Ellen and received her forgiveness.

I have always believed that Ellen was not actually upset about the murder. On the contrary, it pleased her to have such a unique man.

One day they got married. And it was the only day on which I saw Frau Frida Sammet smile. She wore a grey silk dress with black veil, and she babbled like a waterfall. The Perlefter family's gift was a silver centre-piece for fruit.

IX

It was unpleasant for the Perlefter family to have relatives with no virtues; neither fortune, nor talent, nor good manners. I believe that Herr Perlefter suffered much on account of these relatives. For they could not prevent Herr Sammet or his wife from inviting themselves to visit on special occasions. One could not break off relations with this distant part of the family. I have already mentioned a few times that Herr Perlefter did not like severing ties. He had even developed a strong sense of family. If it were up to him he would have been quite happy to chat with Frau Sammet who had known him when he was still an apprentice at a flour concern. Only that no longer depended solely on him. He had many more things to consider than just his family, and one knows how seldom the interests of the world coincide with those of the family.

It was by no means in the interest of the world that Leo Bidak should come together with Perlefter. Nevertheless they came together. Perlefter was not unfriendly. Leo Bidak appeared one afternoon with his young wife. He did not allow her to get a word out. He told stories of Odessa. The young wife was red. He was offered a shot of kümmel, and he drank three. Then he requested some bread and butter, for he ate no sweets. His wife was quite embarrassed.

She had brown skin. When her face was flushed she was pretty. She had narrow shoulders and very wide hips. I already could see that she would bear many children.

And she did have many children. First came twins after only six months. A year later she bore a girl. After four years there were six children, girls and boys, and the whole family lived in the Sammet house.

Old Herr Sammet suffered a stroke. The right half of his body became paralysed. He was in a wheelchair and murmured curses against his wife. The cries of the children stormed through all the rooms, through the corridors and the hall. Leo Bidak's six children seemed like thirty. They broke the banister. They brought stolen cats into the house that gave birth to many litters. Frau Sammet called the children 'bastards'. She suspected the paralysed Herr Sammet was the father. For she was the jealous type.

The young Frau Bidak grew enormously. She always had a round belly, even when she was not pregnant. Her clothes didn't fit her any more, her breasts hung low to the waist, and her brown skin became yellow. She called her husband 'murderer' when she was in a bad mood. And she was often in a bad mood.

One day Herr Sammet suffered his second heart attack and could not be revived. He was buried without tears. I was there, and I saw that the Bidak children were happy. For the first time they wore dark coats and drove in a carriage. The mood was festive as the dead Herr Sammet was buried. Leo Bidak invited the gravedigger to the wake. All the survivors went to the nearest pub and ate and drank until darkness fell. It was summer, and the sun set quite late, and Leo Bidak was drunk and boarded with the whole family into a great Landau. Along the way he bought Chinese lanterns from a street vendor, lit them and caused quite a stir in all the streets through which they drove.

Already on the following day there was a dispute. Leo Bidak didn't want to get up. He was now not only the owner of half the house but also the master of the whole house, and he accepted no more orders from the widow Sammet. He took the dead man's gold coins from their hiding place, showed his aunt and filled his pockets with gold pieces and jingled them around.

The widow replied to this music with fury and grief. She threw a hot flat-iron at her nephew, didn't hit him but instead a bundle of curtains, which caught fire.

Consequently, Leo Bidak went to a factory. He was determined to expand the operations into something 'really big and American'. To this aim, he wanted to purchase large pressing machines. He despised tedious manual labour. He wanted to establish a proper laundry.

He inspected amazing machines. There were some with double tumblers between which the wet laundry was dried, starched and pressed; machines with great wheels that moved independently but which required a great deal of electrical power.

Leo Bidak bought the largest machines of modern design. In the yard of the house he erected a machine room. It took three months to get the machines set up and working. But no good came of it. For the wash came out of the machines half wet, not starched and dully ironed, and the customers were dissatisfied. Leo Bidak's girls had to iron everything again, and it was actually double the work.

At this point, Bidak took out an advertisement in the newspaper and offered the machines for sale. He got rid of them at a huge loss. A technician who had invented a new laundry machine made contact with Bidak who bought the new machine.

Meanwhile many new washerwomen settled in the area and attracted the customers themselves. The meagre assets of Herr Sammet's estate had long since been consumed. Bidak began to take out mortgages on his half of the house.

This steep mortgage, in addition to his other smaller debts, would have embittered him about life had he not possessed such a cheerful nature.

Indeed he had a cheerful nature. His body was ever wider, his belly rounder, his face fuller, his eyes and nose almost entirely disappeared between his cheeks, he gobbled up everything in sight, ate and drank and delighted over every new concern. He did not neglect the upbringing of his children. On the contrary, he gave himself to them quite zealously, and if the results corresponded with his efforts this alone was reward enough.

Leo Bidak had not hit anyone in a long time, and anyone who knows something about wrestlers and athletic nature understands that this talent cannot lie dormant for too long. Bidak would have liked to hit his Tante Sammet. But, for one, he perceived that her withered body offered none of that resistance which provides a joyful inspiration to strike enthusiastic blows; and, second, this Tante Sammet was the only person he began to fear more and more the older and fatter he became.

It was as if the death of her husband had turned on all the sources of venom within Frau Sammet. From a thousand chasms of her soul burst forth this wickedness and thrust itself into the world. It was probably the love that lives longer than one thinks and continues to act when one believes it to be dead and buried – the last remains of her husband's love – which had prevented Frau Sammet from giving vent to the anger and pain housed inside. Now it was unleashed. It was a weary yet unremitting working rage, a woeful doggedness, it was a malice of grief, the distemper of a widow. She went through the house, silent yet audible; she made accusations against no one, but she herself was an accusation; she suffered, she ailed, she looked like a shadow, but she was as only a shadow can be, ever present, frightful and yet not corporeal enough to frighten; she was no longer alive, not of flesh and blood, and therefore eternal, inviolate and immortal. What harm could she do to Bidak's massive body? Her malice gave her a thousand weapons against which health and vigour were defenceless. She muttered curses that one could scarcely hear but that one could feel and therefore began to take effect immediately. She was ever present. She appeared when the children exulted and suffocated their joy, and whenever someone laughed he had to stop suddenly, his laughter broke in the middle like a sparkling glass that suddenly shatters for no apparent reason.

Only Leo Bidak retained his cheerful disposition, as I said before. The bitter, silent fury of his aunt was directed at him, but neither could harm the other. Her terrible wickedness was like a thin steel foil against the heavy armour of cheerfulness that surrounded Bidak. They were two eternal enemies that according to the laws of nature could not counteract one another; they were like day and night, summer and winter, life and death.

Nevertheless Leo Bidak was afraid. He shuddered before the spectre. He did everything possible to annoy his aunt. Actually, he wanted to prove that she was not dead, that she yet lived. He now managed the laundry alone. But on Saturday evenings his aunt came to do the books. He kept her waiting until nine o'clock. Then he went out. At eleven o'clock he returned, and the accounting began. But sometimes Tante Sammet had, one knew not from where, a skeleton key. She figured without Bidak. She could calculate better, and she cheated him out of ridiculous amounts of money. As a rule Bidak came back too late. Then he sought revenge.

His aunt lived on the first floor in a small room.

Bidak locked the door and tied a cat's tail to the handle. The animal cried the whole night through. Nobody in the house could sleep. Only Leo Bidak slept, as he had drunk a great deal. His aunt rattled the door. She broke everything in sight. She shrieked. But Bidak did not hear her. He slept and smiled contentedly in his sleep. Under his pillow lay the key to the door. If his wife attempted to steal the key Bidak awoke; even in his sleep he could detect danger, like an animal.

He soon began to come home early only on Thursdays and Fridays to take stock of the clothing. Half was missing. Customers demanded compensation. Every morning Bidak had to go to court. He hired a number of lawyers. They cost more money than the missing laundry.

And yet Bidak was happy with his life.

I was his truest customer. I had no valuable laundry. It could also have been lost. But my collars and shirts were personally washed and ironed by Bidak. I was not only his truest, I was also the only customer with whom he dealt himself.

We were, one might say, friends. For friendship is a passion like love, it attacks people's hearts and binds two together who march to a different beat, even though they march to a different beat. I must confess at this point that we drank together, went for walks and spoke of various things.

We spoke about sad things, and Leo Bidak understood their full sadness. Yet he smiled. Yes, he even submerged himself completely in the sorrows of the world, and still his mood was cheerful. He was like a sprightly river that rushed through the gloomy deep of a forest, shimmering and alive, yet dark green and dead. He bored himself a loud, joyous path through all terrors.

He not only drank; he also read books but with a preference for the historical. Of all the eras in world history he loved the French Revolution the most. He was a rebel.

If only he were a contemporary of the Revolution! He would have achieved historical glory. For he was not without talent, only without occasion. Nature had not created him to become a laundry owner. He was a noble bandit.

'In the year '48', he said, 'the people of Vienna stood on the city plaza and cried, "Give us Latour!" And they were given Latour. They hung a noose from a streetlamp and strung him up. Why else are there streetlamps in the world? Ha-ha-ha!'

Every day he carried out a thousand little revolutions. He beat up policemen in quiet alleyways, he learned from the statute books and disputed with magistrates and officials, with creditors and notaries, and he argued them into the ground. He read parliamentary proceedings and even gave speeches. For he was an important man in a local chapter of a social democracy group, and on May Day he carried a gold-embroidered red flag.

However, the mortgages beleaguered him, and his half house didn't quite belong to him any more. He now owned but an eighth.

In the summer he arranged a festival in the woods. His children went with him to Knappek's little forest, which he had leased, and he hung lanterns from the trees and surrounded the forest with barbed wire to prevent entry by unauthorized persons without tickets. He worked all day long, but the rain destroyed his paper ornaments, so he brought in new ones. In the middle of a clearing he erected a market tent with lebkuchen, beer and sausages. Two of his children sold cheese. His wife sat at the counter. The presser women gave out beer. During the three days of the proletarian festival Leo's shop was closed.

He personally administered the raffle and the wheel of fortune.

He stood on an empty crate, and to him it was as if he stood on the terrace of a conquered castle. He called out numbers and encouraged the spectators to purchase tickets for the welfare of the proletariat, and he felt like he was giving a rebellious speech to the assembled people.

Then he gave the wheel of fortune a mighty spin. It rattled, squealed and squeaked, and this racket was very pleasing to Bidak, and he smiled so much that his little eyes were no longer visible, and his mouth with its yellow smoker's teeth was wide open, lit by the reddish lantern light, revealing his large red pharynx. Then he gave out the winnings. He always gave the children something, even when they had not won. And as the children didn't usually win Leo Bidak handed out a great deal of money. He paid for these gifts himself.

The local chapter had in Bidak an invaluable member. Thus he soon lost the last eighth of the house.

He sought to get the other half of the house from Tante Sammet. She would not put her signature on the papers. She referred to the fact that she would soon die. Then the other half of the house would belong to the Bidak family anyway.

But Tante Sammet did not die. Death neglected her. He took her for a cat that could not be grabbed. Or perhaps he took her for one of his kind. He did not claim her because she rendered him services. She was temporarily his deputy in the noisy and overly healthy Bidak house. She suffered many accidents. She was tripped, knocked over and had wounds all over her body. A Bidak child threw a fireplace poker at her head.

But she did not die.

X

Bidak was becoming poor, and he was certainly no rich man compared with Perlefter. Neither banks nor professional money lenders, who pay lower taxes than banks and have less obvious signs, could help Leo Bidak. It was at this time that he went to see Perlefter with a little hope in his heart.

When he arrived they had just held a little family gathering to celebrate Fredy's birthday. From what I have already recounted thus far about Perlefter, one already knows that on days which cost him money, even if they brought him joy, he was not especially in the mood to spend still more money on something that would not bring him any pleasure.

. . .

TRANSLATOR'S AFTERWORD

And thus ends the *Perlefter* manuscript, rather abruptly, although at least not mid-sentence. As we begin Chapter X Bidak, in serious need of money, goes to visit his wealthy relative Perlefter. Kroj foreshadows what is about to happen with the last words of that chapter. It is not looking good for Bidak's chances of getting anything out of his indifferent (and tightwad) relative.

Let us assume for a moment that, had the book continued, the following paragraphs would have included a dialogue between Bidak and Perlefter. Now, given that Bidak still needs to leave Europe for America in order for the narrative to catch up with the beginning of Chapter VIII, could this rejection by Perlefter be the plot device that Roth might have used to get Bidak to leave, in frustration and desperation? Who knows, perhaps Perlefter himself suggests that Bidak go to the United States. We know that Bidak has no money, so how does he get to America? Let us imagine the following scenario unfolding at Perlefter's house that day of Fredy's birthday party. Strictly speculation, of course, but perhaps it might have gone something like this:

After Bidak exchanged pleasantries with the rest of the family and offered birthday wishes to Fredy, Perlefter led him into the parlour and gestured for me to follow. We sat and had some schnapps to drink. There was silence for a few moments. At last Perlefter spoke, asking what brought Bidak, although he already knew the answer. As Bidak was alone on this visit it was a serious matter, most likely concerning money.

'I only require a small sum', said Bidak, putting down his glass, 'to keep me from sinking into despair. To prevent me from losing what is left of my half of the house entirely.'

Perlefter told Bidak that there was, of course, no such thing as a small sum. 'This much I have learned being a businessman. Everything adds up!' said Perlefter.

'We are, after all, family!' Bidak said.

'Family indeed,' said Perlefter. 'A large one, at that. And just think if I were to give money to each member of my unwieldy family! Would there be anything left for me? I helped Kroj out years ago, and I'm still not rid of him!' Perlefter gestured at me with his elbow. I knew that he was joking, but I wasn't sure if Bidak took it that way. No, Perlefter did not mind me at all, of that much I was certain. One could say that he tolerated me quite well, considering that overall he had a low tolerance for people. This was certainly true for Bidak. The very fact that Bidak was sitting before him, in his house, was troubling to him. One social visit had already been tolerated, but this, it was most certainly not a social visit. Yes, distance from someone such as Bidak would be quite welcomed.

'You know, I have heard that great opportunities for

an enterprising sort of fellow such as yourself lie across the ocean in America. Those who are down on their luck have seen a great reversal in fortunes over there.' Perlefter forced a grin on to his round face even as he realized the consequences of what he had said. And then the thought struck him. If he gave Bidak money for the here and now, if he helped keep Bidak from losing his part of the house, it was highly likely that he would be back again in no time with some excuse or other to ask for additional funds. This much was certain. A man like this was ill able to hold on to money for more than a few moments. Although it might seemingly cost more to purchase ocean passage for the entire family Perlefter realized that, in the long run, it would result in great savings. He would be rid of Bidak for good, so he thought. A relatively small price to pay.

'But I can't leave,' said Bidak. 'For if I leave I won't inherit the other half of the house when Tante Sammet dies.'

'We are a long-lived family,' Perlefter sighed mightily. 'My father was ninety-two. You will wait in vain. She will not die.' And from the expression on his face it was clear that this confirmed what Bidak was already thinking, what he already knew from experience thus far – that his wicked ghost of an aunt would torment him for many years more.

So, we have thus imagined one possible way that Chapter X might have continued to get Leo Bidak on his way to the United States. I don't expect that Roth would have laid out details of Bidak's years living in San Francisco to the same extent as he already laid out details of his early life, for that would have taken up too much additional space.

Let us assume that Chapter X would have also provided a short summary of Bidak's failed life in the United States, and then presumably in Chapter XI we would have been back to the 'present' of the early 1920s with Bidak's return to Europe at the age of forty-two. He has not arrived at the most opportune time, as Perlefter is in the sanatorium recovering from various 'calamities'. The mere fact that Bidak has returned indicates that he has failed at making a proper life for himself and his family. We must assume that Perlefter and Bidak will meet again. What will their interplay be? Is Tante Sammet still alive? Will Bidak be looking for money once again? Will Perlefter hire him?

And what becomes of Julie? The last we hear of her the dentist is about to become engaged to her. These are questions that are more difficult to answer. Perhaps Roth abandoned this novel when he realized that bringing in Bidak, however interesting a character, had seemed like a good idea but was now limiting how he could handle the remainder of the book. Roth was clearly intrigued by him, having devoted two full chapters and the start of a third to Bidak.

Ultimately, speculation aside, we must take *Perlefter* at face value, just as it was discovered, just as Roth left it in 1929. We can be thankful that we have *Perlefter* and at the same time not too displeased or disappointed that

Roth ceased work on it, because even unfinished it stands as a fine addition to the Roth *oeuvre*.

Besides, while he may not have finished *Perlefter*, he started immediately on another project, a master-piece called *Job*

SOME AUTHORS WE HAVE PUBLISHED

James Agee • Bella Akhmadulina • Tariq Ali • Kenneth Allsop • Alfred Andersch
Guillaume Apollinaire • Machado de Assis • Miguel Angel Asturias • Duke of Bedford
Oliver Bernard • Thomas Blackburn • Jane Bowles • Paul Bowles • Richard Bradford
Ilse, Countess von Bredow • Lenny Bruce • Finn Carling • Blaise Cendrars • Marc Chagall
Giorgio de Chirico • Uno Chiyo • Hugo Claus • Jean Cocteau • Albert Cohen
Colette • Ithell Colquhoun • Richard Corson • Benedetto Croce • Margaret Crosland
e.e. cummings • Stig Dalager • Salvador Dalí • Osamu Dazai • Anita Desai
Charles Dickens • Bernard Diederich • Fabián Dobles • William Donaldson
Autran Dourado • Yuri Druzhnikov • Lawrence Durrell • Isabelle Eberhardt
Sergei Eisenstein • Shusaku Endo • Erté • Knut Faldbakken • Ida Fink
Wolfgang George Fischer • Nicholas Freeling • Philip Freund • Carlo Emilio Gadda
Rhea Galanaki • Salvador Garmendia • Michel Gauquelin • André Gide
Natalia Ginzburg • Jean Giono • Geoffrey Gorer • William Goyen • Julien Gracq
Sue Grafton • Robert Graves • Angela Green • Julien Green • George Grosz
Barbara Hardy • H.D. • Rayner Heppenstall • David Herbert • Gustaw Herling
Hermann Hesse • Shere Hite • Stewart Home • Abdullah Hussein • King Hussein of Jordan
Ruth Inglis • Grace Ingoldby • Yasushi Inoue • Hans Henny Jahnn • Karl Jaspers
Takeshi Kaiko • Jaan Kaplinski • Anna Kavan • Yasunuri Kawabata • Nikos Kazantzakis
Orhan Kemal • Christer Kihlman • James Kirkup • Paul Klee • James Laughlin
Patricia Laurent • Violette Leduc • Lee Seung-U • Vernon Lee • József Lengyel
Robert Liddell • Francisco García Lorca • Moura Lympany • Dacia Maraini
Marcel Marceau • André Maurois • Henri Michaux • Henry Miller • Miranda Miller
Marga Minco • Yukio Mishima • Quim Monzó • Margaret Morris • Angus Wolfe Murray
Atle Næss • Gérard de Nerval • Anaïs Nin • Yoko Ono • Uri Orlev • Wendy Owen
Arto Paasilinna • Marco Pallis • Oscar Parland • Boris Pasternak • Cesare Pavese
Milorad Pavic • Octavio Paz • Mervyn Peake • Carlos Pedretti • Dame Margery Perham
Graciliano Ramos • Jeremy Reed • Rodrigo Rey Rosa • Joseph Roth • Ken Russell
Marquis de Sade • Cora Sandel • George Santayana • May Sarton • Jean-Paul Sartre
Ferdinand de Saussure • Gerald Scarfe • Albert Schweitzer • George Bernard Shaw
Isaac Bashevis Singer • Patwant Singh • Edith Sitwell • Suzanne St Albans • Stevie Smith
C.P. Snow • Bengt Söderbergh • Vladimir Soloukhin • Natsume Soseki • Muriel Spark
Gertrude Stein • Bram Stoker • August Strindberg • Rabindranath Tagore
Tambimuttu • Elisabeth Russell Taylor • Emma Tennant • Anne Tibble • Roland Topor
Miloš Urban • Anne Valery • Peter Vansittart • José J. Veiga • Tarjei Vesaas
Noel Virtue • Max Weber • Edith Wharton • William Carlos Williams • Phyllis Willmott
G. Peter Winnington • Monique Wittig • A.B. Yehoshua • Marguerite Young
Fakhar Zaman • Alexander Zinoviev • Emile Zola